HER
ONLY
FAN

ANDRE SANDERS

CHAPTER ONE

She dropped backwards onto the bed-

BEEERUAAH!

The paper coil on the party horn unraveled and swelled when Ella Pearson puffed one long breath into the plastic piece between her lips. She turned nineteen three months ago but tonight she had her first legitimate birthday bash since coming home from college five weeks ago and getting back in touch with old high school classmates. The night turned irresponsible when she popped the top on the first of many alcoholic beverages, and became more degenerate after she smoked some pot and snorted a few lines of Xanax. She'd never done these things.

Given her current state of mind, interpreting the cream color ceiling spiraling like ice cream out of a long metal dispenser decades before her time, Ella was amazed that she didn't get interrogated about her well being by her mom and stepdad when crossing them in the living room before wobbling her way upstairs. They couldn't have not noticed something was terribly wrong.

Not one word spilled across the room during her sloppy departure.

Ella withdrew the plastic mouthpiece and the paper deflated, coiling instantly. She extended her arm behind her head and let go of the party horn before dragging her hand

1

along the mattress.

The illusion that all her surroundings were spinning became more intense than it was just moments ago. Suddenly her stomach began fluttering.

She closed her eyes.

Even darkness spun.

The flipping and flopping nauseousness within her belly crept into her chest. She believed she might have been able to vomit if not for the Xanax sedating her organs so much to not function properly.

She inhaled deeply.

Exhaled slowly.

The unpleasantness slipped into her throat.

"Oh god," she groaned, and gagged once.

An unexpected belch burned out of her esophagus. The gaseous eye watering stale beer fragrance pushed beyond the powdery residue in her nostrils, resulting in temporary discomfort.

Sitting upright, she rubbed down the front of her face.

Then she stood-

Staggered-

"That's it. I'm done. I'm fucking done," she avowed, referencing her gluttonous consumption of alcohol and inappropriate use of perscription medicine.

Ella shut one eye and squinted the other while looking across the room, and struggled identifying what she knew was there already. Left eye closed, she still saw half the ghost of her wooden desk alongside the physical one. On the desk was a chrome book - opened and powered on.

Stumbling to the desk and leaning over the chair in

front of the computer, she reached down and placed one finger on the built-in touchpad. Ella squinted to acquire a clear view of the monitor. She moved the cursor onto a thumbnail on the far right side of the screen and tapped the touchpad. Suddenly, she was staring at what must have been one hundred small blocks of individual photographs - some with her wearing various styles of bra and panties, but most of them exposed her in the nude - all beneath a large box consisting of only a solid black image. Quite many of those tiny frames revealed a white triangle at the center, meaning they weren't ordinary photographs. These particular icons were likely videos showcasing random performances of *god only knows what* instead.

Ella glanced at the top right corner of the screen, although it was difficult to make out the numbers since she was practically seeing doubles.

1.3k.

96 messages

The top number indicated the total monthly subscribers while the bottom number showed how many unread emails she had from guys, either praising the content or attempting to hit her up for a one night stand. Not looking to waste her time going through those accumulated messages, she swiped the touchpad and moved the cursor into a tiny box connected to the black window positioned above the vast collection of photographs and presumed video clips. Inside this box was the lone, capitalized word PLAY. She tapped the touchpad and the little dark screen dissipated to mirror a familiar scene. The picture displayed her midsection and arm extended with her hand resting idle on the chrome book.

She stepped aside and glanced at the frame without her blocking it and saw that only a portion of the bed was visible. She scrunched her lips, maybe unsure if she was satisfied with the angle, but ended up sliding the cursor into another box that read PLAY.

Opening the top right side desk drawer, she reached inside and retrieved a jaw dropping bright pink silicone dildo. The back of it was round and flat with a bath-ready suction cup. The toy itself was roughly seven inches long - maybe eight. She didn't have big hands but they weren't tiny either; therefore, this monolith of a fuck buddy definitely had the capability to put a hurting inside her.

Smiling, she admired *Pinkie*.

Despite the influx of sensual excitement, she looked at the cursor blinking inside the PLAY box. She took a deep breath, and debated. Could she hold off from doing what she planned and save it for a night when she'd be more mentally involved? Men wouldn't care if she enjoyed the moment or faked her way through the episode; they'd be seeing what they paid for, one way or another.

But…

She was drunk. Aroused. All she wanted to do was fuck herself.

Ella struck the touchpad and the word PLAY suddenly switched to RECORDING. She turned and wandered to the bed, trying to walk as straight as possible because she didn't want guys recognizing how messed up she actually was whenever the session streamed. Along the way, she reached up and fluffed her long black hair to one side of her head. She wanted viewers to get the impression that self pleasure literally roughed her up. Offering the visual representation of manhandling herself would make a dick burst faster than if she dramatized herself in a way too prim and proper.

The first thing did when making her way to the bed was turn and drop backwards. Reaching behind her, she dragged the pillow flat against the headboard so that she would be propped up and able to watch herself on the computer. She felt that it was important to maintain eye contact with the screen because it would help to make the viewer convinced that he was the reason for her getting off.

Ella pressed her shoulders on the pillow and spread her legs with both knees in the air. She gazed provocatively at the computer while pulling the bottom of the shirt up to her titties, but then stalled to prevent exposing them before laying the shaft of pink silicone across her toned stomach. She strained her eyes with a tinge of seduction and eased one hand between her legs. The side of her tongue swiped the corner of her mouth as her fingers slowly maneuvered against the crotch of her booty cut denim shorts. She thrust her hand down until her fingertips grazed the mattress.

Ella groaned rather quietly because she didn't want anyone hearing downstairs. She didn't receive pleasure like she would experience on an ordinary night, but she played along with the awareness that it was all about satisfying the audience.

Firmly pressing the denim, she dragged her fingers up to the top of her midsection and stopped at the waistline to pinch the button but not unfasten it. Her opposite hand slid against her stomach and stumbled upon *Pinkie*. She gripped the silicone base and slowly turned it around with the head pointing at her bellybutton.

"You want this, don't cha?" she asked, loud enough just for the microphone to pick up her voice.

She unfastened the button.

"How bad do you want me?"

Then she slid the zipper down.

"I want you, so … sooo bad."

Slipping *Pinkie* inside the top of her panties, she let out a pretendedly aroused groan as a means to solicit captivation in her eventual audience.

"Don't stop," she insisted.

Ella closed her eyes, trying to imagine-

BAM!

The back of her head smacked the headboard at the same time that darkness inside her mind twirled as if she just stepped away from riding a roller coaster. She recognized that her vision was seriously fucked up but didn't believe bumping her head had any involvement. There wasn't a desk and a half anymore; what suddenly evolved was the desk and an entire phantom replica. For the moment, she couldn't let on that something was seriously wrong with her because she prided herself for having a reputation better than mediocre.

She pushed *Pinkie* further inside her shorts.

If she would have actually felt stimulation, then she might have delivered something more than an amatuer pornstar moan, and her legs would have demonstrated restless anticipation. The strength of substances in her system basically left her suffering with corpse crotch; there was no satisfaction taken from grinding the silicone on her clit.

She thrust her pink pal deeper and squeezed one

breast before letting go and sliding onto the other to do the same. Her eyes did attempt to shut but she struggled to keep them open because she didn't want-

WHAM!

The back of her head collided with the wooden frame. She wasn't aware that her eyes closed until she made contact with the headboard. When she opened them, she found herself plagued with double vision once again. Accompanying it was the visual impression that everything was slowly whirling around her. The inconvenience of not having feeling between her legs spread into her hips and then suddenly surged through the rest of her body so much that she couldn't feel *Pinkie* in her hand.

She looked at what she believed was the real computer but wasn't able to distinguish herself on the screen. It wouldn't have mattered anyway, because the drastic increase of effects she was experiencing, she couldn't pretend anymore.

Ella wasn't aware that she dropped the sex toy.

Her head drifted to one side and almost reached her shoulder before she jerked upright.

"I can't," she mumbled.

Drowsiness was too heavy.

WHAM!

Darkness took its hold on her and refused to give up this time. Ella felt that she was unable to fight the power of sedation towing her deeper into physical and mental incapacitation. She was aware that her head rested against the headboard but she did not have the strength to move forward. Her conscious awareness was becoming less frequent.

Wandered into a place of confusion.

Debilitating numbness gnawed into her head, and the worst feeling to overcome her was having no cognitive understanding of the severity involved with plummeting into the void of silent darkness.

She expired one long breath.

And then committed herself to getting buried alive by those inferior elements.

CHAPTER TWO

Death metal played on the radio but streamed at a relatively low volume. Lights on the dash panel didn't glow bright enough for occupants in the vehicle to see each other's faces clearly. The driver raised what appeared to be a small glass bulb and tube combo. A lighter sparked underneath the bulb and he inhaled while keeping the flame lit on the section of glass darkened by past use.

After taking what he probably suspected was a decent hit, he disengaged from keeping the flame and lowered the lighter to his lap. Then he pulled the glass shaft from his mouth and coughed. White smoke visibly passed the opening in the window rolled down halfway.

He turned toward the passenger with his expression unnoticeable in the dark. "I've fronted you so much shit, man. I don't know if I can do this anymore. You fucking owe me big time, you know that? I'm keeping count of the shit too. You're about three grand in the hole with me."

"I know, dude, and I'm sorry," the passenger admitted. He too was unrecognizable. "I'll get your money. Believe me, I'm working on it. But please… Please help me to get a fix for at least the next couple of days."

The driver gave a noticeable shrug. "I'm not sure, bro. Like I said, I've loaned you way too much as it is and I've not seen a dime."

"I swear, you will get your money. I've got a few lawns lined up. Give me a couple of weeks and I'll work on paying you back," the passenger insisted.

"Some summer landscaping bullshit?!" the driver griped. "That's not gonna pay for shit."

"Come on, man. I'm trying."

"Yeah. You're trying all right. The only thing you're trying to do is take me for a goddamn fool or something," the driver stated.

"No. I told you that I'd pay-"

The driver lunged forward and clocked him in the face. The punch delivered enough force to snap his head back against the passenger window.

"Fuck, Jake!" the passenger shrieked, and cradled his face with both hands.

"I'm no damn idiot, Karsyn. Don't try playing that fucking game with me," Jake barked.

"Dude! I'm not!" Jake shrieked. "Shit! You busted my damn lip."

Jake reached up between them and turned on the interior light. Visibility revealed him to be an older male, probably in his early to mid-forties. Streaks of gray were noticeable in his short dark hair, but it dominated his mustache and goatee. He looked at Karsyn, whose face was still hidden behind his hands. Evidence that he did, in fact, sustain a busted lip was present in a couple of blood drops on his shirt. The driver reached toward the backseat and then came forward with a spare shirt. Karsyn snatched it and pressed it against his mouth.

Jake turned off the interior light. Maybe he didn't want any potential passerbyers eavesdropping on what business he might conduct from this moment onward. Perhaps he simply didn't want to be recognized.

"You gonna be okay?" he asked.

Karsyn patted his mouth. "I'm fine."

Jake leaned over the middle console. "Positive? Because I don't want your mom and dad seeing this and getting themselves involved in shit that's strictly between me and you."

"She isn't my mom," Karsyn stressed. "And they aren't going to say anything. They don't pay attention to the things I do anyway."

Jake glanced at the house across the lawn alongside the curb. "You do know if I was to spot you a little something, then I'm gonna need a little something in return because I can't sit back and wait for you to pay."

"Okay. What do you have in mind?" Karsyn asked.

"Well…" Jake raised a hand to his face but in the absence of light it wasn't clear why. "Let me ask you this; have you ever seen that fine ass sister of yours naked?"

"Oh, hell no!" Karsyn reacted.

"Come on, man." Jake laughed. "You're gonna tell me that you wouldn't go all *Jerry Springer Show* on that shit as long as her mom and your dad didn't know y'all were fucking?"

"God, no!" Karsyn exclaimed. "She's a bitch that thinks she's better than everyone."

"Dude, I'm not saying you've gotta have a relationship with her. It's all about tapping some high grade pussy," Jake stated.

"No. No. No," Karsyn declined. "Even if she wasn't my stepsister, I wouldn't. She isn't my type. Ella comes across as the kind of girl that would just lay there and not get involved."

"All right," Jake replied, staving away from stirring a senseless disagreement based on having a difference of opinion. "What about that beautiful stepmom? What's her name?"

"Blair?" Karsyn inquired.

"Yeah."

"What about her?"

Jake leaned back in his seat and twisted sideways, facing Karsyn. "You ever wanted to get inside her panties?"

"Fuck no, man. That's sick."

"Why not?"

"Why would I have the desire to stick my dick in something my dad's came inside, God knows how many times?"

Jake chuckled. "I'm sure she washes the funk out of that thing on a daily basis."

Karsyn sighed. "Still, nah. She's too much like my actual mom."

Jake reached across and playfully smacked his arm. "Bro, you're living with two hot pieces of ass and you seriously haven't thought once about boning either of them?"

"I haven't," Karsyn replied.

"Okay. Well, I've got an idea," Jake mentioned.

"This should be good. What is it?"

"I'll give you the goods to hold you over for a few days, but you're gonna give me that tight ass sister of yours for a couple of hours. Let me rip that snatch wide open."

Karsyn laughed. "Good one."

"Hear me out. I know how we-"

"Dude, she wouldn't give you the time of day," Karsyn interrupted.

"Listen," Jake continued. "All it would take is for me to give you some good shit that'll knock her the fuck out. She wouldn't know what was happening. She wouldn't remember a thing."

"Whoa… Uh-uh. You're talking about rape," Karsyn stated in shock.

"I don't like referring to it as that," Jake stated calmly. "Willingness to be unwilling is a better term."

"Man, you're out of your fucking mind. That's illegal as shit. I'm not getting myself mixed up in some bullshit situation that risks me being caught or having my name associated," Karsyn said. His voice was still unsettled by the conversation.

"I wouldn't do it at your house, dumbass. No one would know anything," Jake mentioned.

"You're talking some prison sentence bullshit," Karsyn commented.

"The shit you do could send you away for a while."

Karsyn must have acknowledged some truth in that remark because he had nothing more to add. If the wrong person caught wind of his name and snitched him out to authorities, then he'd definitely spend a long unwanted vacation in the state penitentiary for trafficking narcotics. He didn't want to add rape to the list of possibilities that could potentially get him sent away, but Jake did have a valid point in regards to the payment method. Maybe he would have been inclined to make the deal if it didn't pertain to Ella, but since she was the one referenced, he knew he couldn't pretend to not have guilt when seeing her everyday after endangering her.

"All we've got to do is… I'll give you a few pills to crush and slip into whatever drink she's sipping on that day. Go out someplace with her. I don't give a fuck where. Just get her away from her mom. Wait for her to pass out and then swing by my place. I'll fuck her goddamn brains out, and I promise that it won't take me long. When I'm done, then you two can go on your merry way. As far as you and I are concerned, it didn't happen," Jake expressed.

Karsyn slowly leaned back against the headrest and peered into the stretch of darkness beyond the windshield. His mind flashed all the memories of Ella intentionally posing provocatively in front of him, dressed in short shorts and a tank top. Of course, she performed these teases to get a rouse out of him, and he honestly didn't think she was a bad looking girl. Plus she was put together nicely. Just that *"my shit doesn't stink"* attitude was the quality he didn't like.

Suddenly, his memories turned to imagination. He pictured how Ella might look naked, and given the scene transpiring in his head, it was not a pretty sight. Jake was in the image as well. She was bent over the side of a couch with her ass in the air. As much as he didn't want to see Jake naked, he did imagine it. This portentous visualization wasn't the only thing troubling him. He was also able to hear her scream and plead for his interference while he watched from afar. She cried. Groaned in terror. Aggressively swayed her legs on both sides of Jake. She scraped the torn couch cushions with her fingernails but could not pull away. Traumatic suffering bled out of her voice and the only thing he did was stand there and be visually entertained by the ongoing abuse.

Jake treated her more like an animal than a woman. He wrapped her hair around his hand and yanked her head back harder than any woman might enjoy during BDSM rough play. Ella squalled. There really wasn't anything else she could do. When he wasn't pulling hair, Jake was punching areas on her body that he knew would inflict pain. Her agonizing cries were the signature serving as the fact that he delivered those fierce strikes correctly. During the brief periods that he wasn't assaulting her with his hands, she still screamed and pleaded to Karsyn for help. Karsyn wasn't certain but he assumed that Jake was performing dry entry anal sex. It was the only explanation he could come up with to justify her constant anguish.

"Are you down, bro?"

Karsyn vaguely heard Jake's voice from a distance, but he didn't answer. He was too frightened watching and listening to his stepsister get savagely violated.

"Bro!" Jake squawked.

Karsyn snapped out of daydreaming the vivid display, but not until he felt Jake nudge his arm.

"What?" he asked.

"What?!" Jaked mocked. "Dude, are you down for getting me this hookup?"

Those terrible images resurfaced but didn't play out like a movie the way they did just moments ago. Instead, they skipped from one scene to the next like photographs.

"No," Karsyn admitted, emotionally shaken. "I don't think that's a good idea. Fucking with Ella is too risky. If she so much as thought she noticed a cum stain in her panties, then she'd go running to her mom and throw that shit on blast."

"Aww," Jake blurted out. "You're in love with her, aren't you?"

"Hell nah," Karsyn retaliated.

Jake laughed. "All right. If you're not gonna give me a shot at that one, then how about we schedule a little get together with that sweet ass mom?"

"Man, seriously?!" Karsyn blasted. "How is that any different?"

"Less risks involved," Jake stated.

"Less risks? How do you figure that?"

"For one, you wouldn't have to be seen in public with her. We can do everything right there in the comfort of your home."

Karsyn shook his head with a level of disagreement that was noticeable in the dark. "Still isn't a good idea."

"Listen to me before you bash what I haven't said," Jake argued.

Understanding that his persistent disapproval would instigate a verbal confrontation, Karsyn didn't respond.

Which led Jake to lay out his alternate plan. "I can give you the pills to spike her drink after your dad leaves for work. Wait for them to take effect and then call me as soon as she passes out. I'll get here as quick as I can, bust a nut, and then bounce out like nothing happened. I'm sure your dad probably hits it every night; so, you wouldn't have to stress about her freaking over finding cum stains in her underwear."

Karsyn lowered the shirt from his mouth and slung it to the backseat. "Dammit, Jake. What part of *that's still rape* do you not understand? I'm not okay with any of it."

Jake raised his hand and dangled a tiny ziplock bag with two fingers. Inside the bottom of the bag appeared to be some type of powdery substance. There wasn't much in quantity but the amount didn't matter because the only thing that truly concerned Karsyn was the quality.

"You're taking a big risk, bro. I get the pussy and you get the Chalk. That's how it works. All it takes is for you to agree and I'll hand this over to you right here, right now," Jake encouraged.

Karsyn discovered that his mind wandered into terrain inhabited by Blair. He wasn't surprised to find her completely nude. Jake was in the scene as well. Naked, again. The one major difference compared to those horrible concepts regarding Ella was that Blair wasn't bent over the junkyard ugly arm of a filthy couch in the despicable perimeters of Jake's residence.

She was crying, though, and constantly yet unsuccessfully trying to drag herself from the clutches of unethical sexual behavior. Her petrifying requests for some form of intervention seemed to fall on deaf ears.

Karsyn stood in the doorway and watched the violent assault unfold on her own kitchen table. Blair laid on her back with both legs locked around Jake's hips while he gripped the sides of her thighs to prevent her from squirming loose and potentially getting away.

Based on the intense cycle of thrusts, Jake was being overly aggressive during penetration. Blair wailed each time that he rammed forward against her. She arched her head back, looking at him observing them from the doorway. Recognizing him caused her to scream louder and more frequently as tears streamed down her face. She jerked one side of her body off the table but the desire to fight back didn't last for long because fatigue caused her to drop onto the table again.

Aggravated with her disobedience, Jake let go of one thigh to reach up and grab her throat. He had evidently applied profound force because she went from screaming and groaning to choking and whispering inaudibly. Loss of oxygen eventually gave her face a pastel purple complexion.

Jake's wild grunting became the only sound in the situation. Karsyn stared at the panic in her eyes and felt as if her unappeasable gaze penetrated him.

Aghast by his own thoughts, Karsyn escaped his imagination entertaining him with morbid scenery. He looked at the bag between him and Jake and his heavy heart weighed the dismal risks of agreeing to a deal.

"Nah. I know I've said I can't stand her for taking my mom's place, but she's a human like both of us, so is Ella. I'm not down with doing anything that fucked up."

"Suit yourself." Jaked snatched the bag up in his hand and concealed it.. "Only thing you had to do was work something out."

"Come on, man," Karsyn urged.

"I tried to do things where it would help you and myself. You want this shit, and I wanna bust a goddamn nut. But if you ain't willing to help me see that happen, then I ain't no help to you," Jake specified.

"There's got to be another way," Karsyn insisted.

"Oh, there is." Jake twisted forward and pressed his back on the seat, before reclining the backrest and making himself cozy. "I'm just not sure if you'll fancy it over those things I've already stipulated."

Karsyn leaned back and pressed the passenger door. "For fuck sake, dude. I'm not giving you a handjob."

Jake chuckled. "Did I mention anything about getting jerked off?"

"No but what you're saying …"

"What am I saying?"

Karsyn didn't answer him straight away. Perhaps he was confused about where the conversation had gone. But then, finally he replied, "I don't know."

"Right. I don't want some cheap ass handjob. What I want is a fucking blowjob."

"Goddamn, man! What the hell are you tripping on?!" Karsyn shrieked. "I'm not sucking your dick for shit?"

"Nothing wrong with just talking about it." Jake leaned forward and reached underneath the seat. When he raised back and made himself comfortable again, he positioned his hand in the space between his legs. "But you can't sit here and tell me that you've never sucked cock. I recall there being a few instances that you gave head. For what? All for the same reason you're sitting here now, wanting shit from me that'll fuck you up for a while. Right?"

"Jake, bro, it's not like that. I didn't volunteer myself to do anything. I was totally messed up when that shit happened. Dammit, I passed out one of those times."

"How bad do you want this Chalk?" Jake asked, and at no point did his tone resonate with humor.

"Holy fuck. You're serious, aren't you?"

"Have you ever known me to bullshit you?"

"Dude, no. To hell with this. It's pretty fucking sick you thought I'd stoop that low."

Jake raised his hand from between his legs. Karsyn couldn't identify the model but distinguished that a handgun was what he had reached under the seat and retrieved. Jake didn't seem shy about making the weapon noticeable because he lifted it high enough in front of him to align with the steering wheel.

Click.

The horrible sound of the hammer getting cocked did not go unheard.

"Really?! A fucking gun! You're going to pull this shady bullshit on me?!" Karsyn shrieked.

Jake pointed the weapon at him. "If I want something bad enough, then I'm gonna get it. Doesn't matter how far I've gotta go either."

"Put that thing away, Jake. We can go up the road and find you something a lot better. I'm sure there are some little whores flaunting their skank asses at the park."

"I stated what I wanted but you didn't agree. Now we're gonna do the alternative."

"No way, man. I don't care what you think you know or have heard about me but I am not doing that."

Keeping the gun pointed at his face, Jake extended the weapon in close range above the console. "You'll do what I say or I'll unload the clip on your face, and you know better than anyone that I don't give a damn to do it right here."

"You're out of your fucking mind."

"Get over here," Jake snapped, scooting down and

pushing his lower half forward. "I'm about five seconds from pulling the trigger."

"Let's figure something out," Karsyn pleaded.

"Five. Four…"

"Shit! Okay! Okay."

Jake didn't let his guard down but did retract from aiming too close.

"Never tell anyone about this," Karsyn insisted, slowly leaning across the console and reaching both hands toward Jake's midsection. "I cannot believe this is happening."

"No one ever has to know a thing. As far as I'm concerned, this stays between you and I," Jake mentioned.

Karsyn unfastened the belt in a hurry because he wanted the ordeal over with and beyond him. Undoing the button and sliding the zipper down, Karsyn unfolded the flaps of the jeans and exposed the boxers underneath.

Jake sighed as though pleased. "Yeah… Come to daddy."

Karsyn closed his eyes.

Dread and misery intensified.

He didn't want to see it all transpire and serve as a horrible recurrence in his memory.

Easing one hand inside the boxers, his fingers brushed along the disgusting field of rough pubic hair. Didn't take but a couple of small strides until he fumbled across the sweaty texture of flaccid meat hanging between the legs. He grabbed what felt like its entire length. One quick bend of the wrist nudged the boxers away from hiding what Karsyn vowed not to observe.

He couldn't believe what he was about to do, but he

understood that he had no other option. He realized the seriousness in Jake's demand when the gun got brought into the matter. He had never known Jake to be the kind of guy who didn't mean what he said; therefore, he was terribly conscious of the fact that he either suck the dick or become a soon forgotten somebody in Virginia's homicide statistics. At twenty years old, he was prepared to preserve his longevity at all costs.

Lowering his face toward Jake's lap brought him to terms with an odor that he'd never come across. This awful scent had to be the result of stale sweat and hygiene deprivation. Jake's appearance didn't actually present a man who took proper care of himself because his face and hands revealed grime during the little bit of time that he was visible in the light. Karsyn could not fathom that he was going to insert this rancid smell inside his mouth.

Not wanting to do anything that might potentially signal disagreement and excite Jake's trigger finger, he devoured the clammy penis down to the wiry pubes poking all around his mouth. The initial taste repelled him so much that he gagged.

The injured portion of his lip burned while scrubbing spit covered skin. He raised but then stopped when the heat of the penis brushed the back of his teeth.

"Dammit, boy," Jake groaned. "I'm gonna have to swing by here and see you more often."

Karsyn didn't speak. Then again, he wasn't capable. He knew if he attempted, then all that would have come out was a gurgle here and a gargle there. Preferring to remain quiet, he slid the entire shaft inside his mouth. He felt increased blood flow pulse through veins as the erection swelled on his tongue.

One thing out of his control was the fact he drooled everywhere. Saliva smeared all around his mouth and drizzled to his chin. He tried wiping it off with the back of his hand but there was so much that he only managed to wet his hand without clearing his face.

"Ahh, yeah. Don't stop. I'm almost there," Jake affirmed.

Karsyn paused.

The phrase *almost there* bore an ominous meaning to something that he wasn't prepared to endure.

But it seemed that Jake was determined to have him experience the incident anyway. Karsyn felt him press one hand on the back of his head and push until the head of the cock plugged his airway. Jake thrust himself off the seat and plunged what Karsyn felt was another inch deeper in his throat. Then he lowered slowly and relaxed in the seat again.

Pushed.

Relaxed.

Pushed.

Difficulty breathing caused his eyes to water as if he was crying. Having his airway blocked did cause him to gag, several times. Every effort to breathe through his nose didn't help since it was partially buried in the bristly fluff of pubic hair.

Then it happened.

Jake squirmed beneath him before an abundance of warm goo splattered his tonsils and lodged in his esophagus. Karsyn began choking, and tried prying himself upward; nevertheless, Jake continued pressing his head which immediately halted his effort to pull away. He did the only thing he knew to do in the situation and that was force himself to gag and hurl the unwanted gob of semen forward. Freed from choking, he spilled all the warm jizz onto Jake's cock.

Suddenly, Karsyn was let go.

Perhaps he fulfilled every decrepit desire leading up to the moment that Jake ejaculated.

He removed himself and swiped a few fingers through the middle of the slimy string that connected to his mouth and Jake's midsection.

"What the hell, man?!" Jake squalled. "You're gonna get me off and leave this fucking mess?!"

Karsyn slumped back in the passenger seat. He apparently had nothing to say in regards to that aspect of dissatisfaction.

Jake chuckled and reached to the backseat, retrieving the same filthy shirt that Karsyn used to apply pressure on his lip. Fresh blood seemed not to be an issue since he unraveled the shirt without analyzing its stains, and proceeded to wipe hard against his genitalia.

"You did good, kiddo. Better than any strung out bimbo that I ever shacked up with in my twenties. Don't let it rev your ego though; I'd much rather have your scrawny ass sister on my dick."

"Stepsister," Karsyn exhaled.

"What the fuck ever." Jake yanked his boxers up and tossed the shirt on the backseat. Then he flicked the small ziplock bag onto Karsyn's lap. "You upheld your end of the bargain, and I'm a man of my word. You do still owe me for all the times I fronted you, but I'll try to be less aggressive about it since you did just go above and beyond."

Karsyn nodded and nothing more.

He bowed his head before picking up the bag. That small amount of powder in the bag caused him to feel repulsed and infuriated. Jake may have forced him to commit the act but he was responsible for getting himself embroiled in such indecency by sinking too deep in an addictive lifestyle.

What lingered as a reminder that his life preserved no moral value was the salty aftertaste from giving head. He could also sense the unsavory fragrance of greasy cock in saliva that had dried and stained around his mouth.

No uplifting thoughts followed the outcome.

Chaotic negativity was the lone illness which insisted on being his inimitable companion.

Deterioration.

Embarrassment.

Regret.

All of these feelings interlaced with his momentary hatred toward Ella and Blair for their erogenous existence contributing to him getting shamefully face-fucked; however, the next moment there was supreme resent toward himself for banishing what little dignity he thought he conserved after years of prominent stupidity.

But then…

He felt a complete and sudden change in his state of being. Every weight of negativity altered into a bizarre form of adrenalin that only the narcotic hungry fiend inside him could understand.

The voice inside his head *seeking a fix* assured him

that it was appropriate to conduct a personal sacrifice during instances of desperation, and it sort of flirted by reminding him about the high he would get after sniffing a line.

Karsyn squeezed the tiny bag of *Chalk* inside his fist. The only thought on his mind at this point was to get to his bedroom, kick back, and slice a line.

All while temporarily embracing the motto-

Fuck everyone.

And everything.

CHAPTER THREE

Adult life in the Undergrove household, given Cody's surname for the reason that he took Blair and Ella into his home prior to this second marriage, seemed to persist with going about its typical routine. Blair sat in the leather recliner and concentrated on the true crime episode broadcasting on the television. Her nighttime attire was a tank top and pajama pants patterned with characters from the *Rugrats* cartoon. Something in her physique was offset. Blair's slender shoulders and average build didn't match her abnormally large stomach protruding further than her breasts. Could it be that she was pregnant? The visual response was, yes. She was due to burst at any moment.

Cody sat on the end of the couch furthest from Blair. His skinny jeans and button-up shirt were an insinuation that he didn't plan to hit the bed any time soon. With one leg crossed on top of the other and both hands on his lap, he was undeniably absent from the television program while submerging himself in content displayed on his mobile phone.

"I'm interested to know why you didn't demand testimony from that rebellious daughter of yours about what her involvements were tonight," he said, without glimpsing in her direction.

Blair didn't give an instant response because she

carefully considered her choice of words. She lived with Cody long enough to be fully aware of his narcissistic intelligence to twist their conversations for his argumentative leverage, and she was aware that one wrong word could ignite an out of control reaction.

Finally, she replied. "I didn't feel tonight was the proper time to question her latest activities."

"Did you not notice she was hardly able to walk?" he questioned, staying fixed on the phone.

"I saw," she answered.

"And you're just going to sit there and condone that behavior?"

Blair sighed. She knew what was happening and where he projected this conversation to go. He was verbally phishing for a simple disagreement to set off a chain of intentional misunderstandings which would result in them having a ridiculous argument which he would cleverly pronounce his way to victory. Nothing in his old tricks ever changed. She wised up in identifying his tactics and put herself in the position to play his game by having his pathetic overbearing ego believe that it had one.

"No, Cody. I do not condone her bad decisions. I didn't say anything to her tonight because it would have gone over her head and totally forgotten about in the morning. I'll preach to her tomorrow and make sure she realizes that we will not tolerate or allow such disrespect for as long as she's living under our roof."

This peaceful tactic to euthanize the megalomaniac inside him seemed to reach a successful conclusion in the way that he apparently had nothing more to add on the matter.

Blair knew deep down that she wasn't going to say anything to Ella about tonight because she also went through phases of harmless disobedience at Ella's age. Her parents never snapped and jumped down her throat for any of them either. Cody didn't grow up portraying to be some perfect little angel himself. He shared many stories with her about how he caused his parents much grief during his late teens to early twenties. He allegedly did things that involved him receiving an underage possession of alcohol charge to experimenting with cocaine, but she didn't know how much truth existed in these boisterous self proclamations. Despite the potential if what he said was fact or fiction, she wasn't going to stand down and allow his inflexible standards to influence how she raised her daughter. She believed that she had done a decent job as a mother prior to him entering their lives; therefore, she was not inclined to give him authority to conduct the methodology of their *thicker than water* relationship.

Fortunately, the ability to falsely impress went far in the Undergrove household.

If Cody was happy, then all of them could rest assured that they didn't have to proceed the day with caution.

He lost himself quietly in the abstract reality of content pulicized on his mobile phone. There were multiple thumbnail photographs set forth on a black backdrop. Identifying features of the model involved weren't detectable since the images exhibited themselves too small on the phone screen. The only thing he distinctly recognized was the various styles of which she presented herself. Each picture revealed her in a different pose with every piece of lingerie not the same as the ones modeled prior. Some photographs showed her lying on a bed. Other photos exposed her fully naked.

While not one of those images could raise suspicion on his potential association with the model in question, there was an eerie name at the top of the page that might creepily indicate to be a red flag. The unique hot pink title *Ella_Bare69xox* spanned in large font across the top of the page.

If Blair had been in proximity and glanced at his phone, then she probably would have become unnerved upon noticing the name linked to this adult content was identical to the stepdaughter whose life he seemed to excessively enjoy making difficult.

Cody began scrolling down the page but then paused and tapped a random thumbnail. The display switched from showing the compilation of thumbnails to going fullscreen with the particular image that he chose. The picture advertised an up close recognition of the young model's unmistakable characteristics.

This photograph was chilling evidence of a true nightmare that an adoring mother likely wasn't aware existed.

This image was also damning testimony that Cody secretly incubated a personality trait much darker than all the flawed attributes known about him already.

It was utterly impossible for him to not know the model in the photo was the same Ella living under his roof. The layout of the bedroom in the background verified this revelation as well. His interest in reviewing her productivity may have been less bizarre if it was a common image, but this was anything except ordinary. Ella went the distance to disguise her youth beneath heavily applied makeup which did appear quite successful in portraying her as a whore. Her bottom attire was a blue lace thong. The only thing protecting her breasts was her hands pressed against them. Her lips were puckered in the sense that she was ready to give a kiss. Ella had gone for the provocative expression and she certainly delivered on the effort.

Above her naughty pose was a stretch of glowing hot pink words that came together to form the question-

Daddy wanna hit me?

For her to have posted that on her end of the spectrum was as evenly disturbing as him snooping through her content.

Was something freakishly intimate going on between Ella and her asshole for a stepfather? Or could it just be a subliminal message on her behalf to give awareness that she knew he browsed the page?

The possibility of her knowing about his heterodox pervertedness didn't push him to abandon. Instead, he made an unusual move by going to the bottom of the screen and pressing a small box that stated the recommendation to provide her with a tip. This apparently wasn't his first journey to the generous gift section of her account because all of his credit card information was listed in its appropriate spaces after the page loaded. The only blank section on the entire documentation dealt with how much of a tip he wanted to give. There were three blocks with a preset amount in each and he could choose just one. Five dollars. Fifteen dollars. Twenty dollars. He tapped the middle option and a verification box popped up for him to agree and accept the terms of the transaction.

He pressed accept.

Transaction cleared.

The verification box disappeared.

The page refreshed but took him all the way back to the beginning. Again, the top of the screen brandished the large and vibrant: *Ella_Bare69xox*. Having to do the process all over again, he swiped one finger up the screen and began scrolling down the page. He passed the photo that he had clicked and tipped and continued to bypass uncountable thumbnails without hesitance.

The page display was much different on his phone than how things were laid out on Ella's chrome book . This became apparent after passing several more columns of thumbnails and reaching a second set of image files titled Media Clips. He stopped scrolling after coming upon this series of files and gave each one equal attention while trying to decide which of these videos might be most entertaining. They all seemed to offer a different scenario. Some images showed her laying on the bed and ready for action with *Pinkie*. Other media thumbnails displayed Ella dressed in lingerie and standing in front of the camera. He assumed these were episodes of her performing strip teases. There was one image of her standing in the bathroom; likely this pertained to her giving a quick strip and recording herself taking a shower.

Before getting himself more involved by watching one of these clips, he pressed the volume control button on the side of the phone and watched the indicator drop all the way to mute after. He obviously didn't want Blair hearing any potential sound. Would be impossible to explain why he was watching a video that streamed Ella's voice with Blair not able to watch it with him.

He glanced at Blair and saw that she was deeply involved in trying to decide who did what on the television show. But then, he assumed that she never paid him much attention anyway. He supposed that he could sit there all night and view every bit of Ella's content without her interrupting to ask what he found thoroughly interesting enough to be so extensively time consuming. After double checking that the volume was muted, he clicked one of the icons and it went fullscreen to advertise Ella wearing skimpy lace lingerie in front of the camera.

He glimpsed at Blair again and saw that she was still oblivious to his actions.

His finger slid to the center of the screen and tapped the *Play* symbol practically covering Ella's entire stomach. Luckily, the icon disappeared when the clip began playing. The footage started with Ella just standing in front of the camera for a moment. He did notice her mouth moving which confirmed him having good reason to kill the volume because the situation definitely would have become not just embarrassing for him but also potentially threatening to the longevity of his marriage.

The video continued for a few more seconds with Ella standing in place and apparently talking to the camera. Cody could only imagine the words coming out of her mouth were filthy and self-degrading. Suspecting her to be acting this way somewhat aroused him before the segment steered toward unraveling its nature as a visually enticing production.

She leaned forward and reached out of frame. Then

she stood and brought her hand in front of her again. Expecting things to heat up quickly, he wasn't surprised to see her holding *Pinkie*. He squirmed once because it bothered him - not in a bad way - when the notion struck that she was achingly preparing to drive the flab of silicone flesh insensitively fast inside herself just to get off without a second wasted.

Blair peeked at him long enough from the corner of her eye to recognize his brief adjustment. She evidently paid more attention than he realized. She abstained from questioning what he found enticing after acknowledging his momentary burst of excitement. She was used to seeing him distracted and vaguely aware of whatever situation taking place around him. Not surprisingly, she diverted her attention back on the television with the intent to de-escalate what might otherwise propel a casual conversation into a verbal catastrophe. Of course, she would have had every right to argue if she knew the circumstance, but her ignorance of the matter made her feel that causing a scene would lead to her coming across as being childish and attention starved. Cody had been meticulous about manipulating arguments and portraying himself as the victim in the past.

He continued to watch the video and eagerly anticipated witnessing how far Ella was willing to go after slowly walking backwards to the bed and rubbing *Pinkie* from between her breasts to her stomach, circling the tip of the silicone head around her belly button.

Although he was significantly involved with the content on his phone, Cody did hear the door open behind him.

WHAM!

The nasty disruption of it slamming shut fired across the room.

Cody pressed one of two buttons on the side of his phone and the screen immediately went dark. He obviously did this to prevent wandering eyes from peeking over his shoulder to find him entertaining himself with the naughty nature of his stepdaughter.

Karsyn crossed alongside the end of the couch nearest his father. He glanced down and noticed the inactive phone but what intrigued him was the strange manner in which his father avoided contact as if waiting for him to move along.

He glimpsed at Blair and saw her looking at him. She pulled her hands against the bottom of her swollen belly before moving her lips in the sense that she wanted to speak, but she didn't say anything. Perhaps she refused to say whatever came to mind for the reason of not wanting to provoke Cody to provide some unnecessary smartass remark. At the moment, Karsyn did want the acknowledgement from one of them and he didn't care if it transpired from Blair's considerate attribute or his father's snide disposition. Positive or negative, both would be affirmation that they validated his subsistence. He craved their attention. Needed their approval.

Cody never once looked at him.

Blair still had nothing to say but she did pitch a slight nod while rubbing one hand across her stomach. Karsyn wasn't quite sure what she meant by signaling this gesture; however, he accepted it to be an expression of half ass recognition and did with it what was probably expected.

He returned the courtesy with equal poor effort and embarked on the same misguided journey as Ella.

BOOMP!

Boomp!

The sound of his stomps resonating throughout the living room lessened as he ascended the stairs.

Cody pushed the same button on the side of his phone that he nudged earlier and the screen turned on again. The frozen display showed Ella clad in lingerie and halfway on the bed. He poked the screen with one finger and the video began playing. Ella planted her ass on the bed and scooted toward the headboard while focusing on the webcam. Her knees pointed upward after she curled her legs in front of her chest, but then she spread them beyond her sides and slowly rubbed the dildo from the inner side of her knee up to the crease of her thigh.

Blair fired another glance at him. "Do you ever wonder what he's got himself involved in to be out so late and have random strangers show up in front of the house every night?"

Cody didn't respond. He couldn't because he was too mesmerizingly mind fucked with anticipation to see what else Ella was going to reveal.

"Earth to Cody," she uttered.

He sighed and tapped the screen which happened to pause the segment at the exact moment that Ella brushed *Pinkie* onto the bottom center of the thong.

Then he glanced rather undesirably at Blair. "What's your deal?"

"What's my deal?" she whispered, treading carefully by asking the same question for the fact that she didn't want their exchange to turn sour. "You're concerned about what Ella does and if I'm going to handle matters properly; so, I'm curious if it interests you to know Karsyn's involvements and if you plan to handle the situation if it is, in fact, not in his best interest."

Cody smirked. "That boy is old enough to take care of himself. He and I also established a long time ago that whatever trouble he gets himself into, then it's up to him and him alone to resolve."

"What makes you think that Ella can't take care of herself?" she asked.

He shrugged. "She's just a young stupid girl, Blair. Wouldn't take much from a prick with a stiff dick to talk her into doing whatever he wanted, and she would not second guess herself. Before you know it, that girl would have herself in some deep shit."

"I beg your pardon, Cody; she is way more responsible than the credit you give her," Blair addressed, flirting with the danger of their conversation becoming confrontational.

He looked at his phone and smiled while envying the exhibit of silicone pressed between her legs. "I've got the impression that she is more trouble than she's worth. Probably doing all sorts of inappropriate shit that would appall you, if you knew."

"I know my daughter quite well," she added. "She has better judgment than to go out and get herself messed up with the likes of some immature dickhead."

"Maybe it's Ella that you should be concerned about more than who she runs around with," he mentioned.

She rolled her eyes at his remark. "Why do we even

bother having these discussions? We never agree on anything. To be honest, neither of us pay enough attention to know what they're doing or where they are most of the time."

Cody struck the screen and the video began playing. Satisfaction increased amongst his hunger when Ella shifted *Pinkie* to the side of the thong and nudged its fabric to the center of her private. She didn't completely expose herself but showed a decent amount of flabby skin which didn't leave much for the imagination to consider.

"Believe me, I see more than you know," he stated.

Then he giggled.

His deep seeded asshole persona, combined with attributes of narcissism, prompted him to feel ecstatic during the quick release of grim endorphins - triggered by some false sense of godliness resulting from the predatory desire to witness his stepdaughter behave badly while her clueless mother sat in close proximity.

CHAPTER FOUR

Karsyn had coated the bristles on his toothbrush with a thick mound of paste but it failed to eliminate the phantom taste of dirty flesh and salty semen as recollections of the incident ran fresh in his mind. On top of being reminded how foul the taste was, he also felt physically grimy. The outcome of the incident left the deeply troubling impression that he'd been maliciously face raped - which, in fact, was not far from the truth.

He spit in the shallow puddle of water circling the drain. His saliva was bright blue as a result of the paste but there was also a trace of red swirls. Evidently, he scrubbed his gum too hard. Unbothered by the aggressiveness, he stuck the lightly stained head of the brush back inside his mouth and proceeded to sweep across his teeth just as swiftly and vigorously as when he started.

He looked at his reflection and saw how careless he had become in treating himself. Saliva, laced with paste and blood, caused a foam eruption of almost pink bodily fluids to skim past his lip and ooze toward his chin. He tried slurping the spillage back inside his mouth but was only able to partly succeed before being forced to bend forward and spit again. When he raised and checked himself in the mirror, he noticed a red outline trace where every tooth embedded in the flesh. The pink stain made

39

from blood and paste spread across his teeth. The pink stain made from blood and paste spread across his teeth.

Suddenly, he wasn't aware of the situation because he became mentally absorbed in private knowledge of a past involvement.

The recollection arrived in black and white. Perhaps the actual event transpired in the dark and there was no better way to remember it. Apparently, it didn't matter because he seemed capable of recalling the experience as if it had happened in broad daylight.

The circumstance unraveling inside his head didn't just show him on a bed but revealed him on top of the bare chest of a woman whose face his remembrance concealed. He saw himself kissing her breasts, circling their nipples with his tongue until they hardened enough for him to give each a few delicate nibbles. She seemed to enjoy his assertive handling of her body based on the passionate yet somewhat subtle groan that embraced them both before her hands reached the sides of his head and coursed through his hair with no genuine sense of direction.

Karsyn observed himself maneuver lower on her body until his head occupied the gap between her legs. He couldn't recall her taste but one significant trait did resurface. How the exhilarating region of her body - thick, soft, and damp - felt against his mouth was unforgettable. He remembered how his tongue dipped inside her for so long that the skin glazed over with arousal; conformed to emanate the finest bittersweet earthly fragrance.

The woman groaned.

Gasped.

Spewed his name in one breath.

He noticed his memory was arousing him as much as he'd been physically alert during the actual encounter. The fast developing throb in his pants craved a material recurrence.

"Mmmm ... Oh, baby."

The relaxed and concupiscent tone of her voice intimately haunting his thoughts almost caused him to ejaculate without touching himself.

The well detailed flashback of providing her with an adequate amount of oral pleasure unexpectedly altered to present him standing at the foot of the bed while she lay pulled to the edge. They were still cast in black and white, with her identity remaining out of sight. Her legs were raised and wrapped around his lower back. Both of his arms were extended forward and his hands squeezed the width of each breast. He thrust back and forth fiercely, potentially aspiring to overcome her with an enjoyment unlike anything she ever received.

The sounds ricocheting inside his head were an impressive tease.

The faster his repetitions of driving his dick inside her, the louder she groaned. She also began to call out his name. When she wasn't being vocal, it seemed she expressed minor difficulty breathing.

On the cusp of reminiscing their charismatic energy become expelled through mutually vitalizing orgasms, he surprisingly identified that he was banished from eavesdropping on the astounding climax because he had been diverted to seeing his reflection stare back at him.

He pulled the toothbrush from his mouth before leaning forward and spitting. Then he reached the foam stained brush under the faucet and cleansed it, only to stick it in his mouth again and suck what little amount of water the bristles absorbed.

He spit.

Rinsed. Sucked. Spit.

He repeated the steps until his spit showed almost no trace of blood. Afterwards, he placed the toothbrush in a little round opening on the lid of a cup style holder with three other brushes that likely belonged to Cody, Blair, and Ella - under the assumption they all shared the same bathroom.

Putting the sides of his hands together and reaching under the faucet, he pulled away cradling water before splashing his face. Then he raised and looked at himself in the mirror and saw the shimmer on his skin replaced the foam bubbles.

He shut the water off and dried his hands on a bath towel draped inside the ring of a circular wooden hanger on the wall beside him. Then he patted his face.

Karsyn opened the door while reaching in his pocket and feeling the sealed edge of the plastic bag brush his fingertips. He stalled in the doorway after turning the light off and looked at the closed door to another room across from him. Temporarily uncertain of his thoughts, he glanced at the side of the hallway that dead ended but was open on the left side at the top of the staircase. Maybe he was keeping an eye out for the most vague shadow movement, while carefully listening to identify the slightest sound that would signal if either Cody or Blair was creeping up the steps. It was getting late and neither of them ever stayed up for too long; however, tonight their routine seemed unordinary because he didn't hear any commotion outside the door when he was in the bathroom, and he didn't pick up on any indication that they were ready for bed when he stepped inside the house.

Assuming he had plenty of time to do whatever was going through his mind, Karsyn took one long stride across the hallway and stood face to face with the door. He grabbed the front of his pants and pushed and pulled as if trying to position his potentially embarrassing boner in a way to be unnoticed. Then he raised his hand to knock but paused before making contact. Still perplexed about what was in his intent since he didn't actually know, he withdrew from what would have resulted in a quick tap and reached for the handle.

He twisted the knob.

Hesitated.

Perhaps he was struggling in his confused mind about how to confront the other side.

He was aware that he didn't have all of the time in the world to figure it out because he pushed the door open soon after the pause. What greeted him was the most unexpected sight. The glow from the lamp on the nightstand shone across Ella laying on the bed. She was passed out and in such a deep sleep that he could hear her snoring from the doorway. What he thought was unusual was her peculiar presentation; shirt raised with tits exposed and shorts unfastened. He couldn't see *Pinkie* since the silicone behemoth was laying on her opposite side, but if he did, then he would have recognized that his finding was minimally bizarre in comparison to what he should have discovered if she hadn't failed.

Being her stepbrother, Karsyn believed he should feel disgust for viewing her half naked, but he didn't. Instead, he sensed the compelling urge to prolong his observation and absorb every little detail.

Still fondling the small bag in his pocket, he felt excitement shift the erection toward his hand.

He looked across the room and noticed her computer was turned on. Not only did he recognize that but also saw the screen displayed an image box which broadcast Ella asleep on the bed. Recognizing this didn't take long for him to figure out the webcam was recording for whatever reason.

He looked at her on the actual bed again. His interest in her stiff nipples made him want to step over and caress the breasts before slipping one hand inside the open folds of her shorts. He had never thought about Ella in a sexual nature, but seeing her partly exposed left him unable to avoid the temptation to fantasize. The fact that she wasn't in the condition to remember any unnecessary act that he could easily perform on her made his enthusiasm to explore more desirous. Having a boner which craved making a mess of good feminine hygiene didn't help the situation either. Fortunately, he dug deep inside himself and mustered enough moral reasoning not to react to the ache.

Rather than do what might be deemed most appropriate; such things that involved walking over and turning the computer off before going bedside to cover Ella with a blanket and turn the lamp off, he reacted as though he never interrupted. He nudged the erection away from his pocket and quietly pulled the door shut after taking a step back.

He glanced down the side of the hallway resulting in a dead end and briefly listened this time before turning and walking in the opposite direction. Stopping in front of the last door on the left side of the hall, he pulled the bag from his pocket and was immediately aware of the reason that he had gone to Ella's room. The idea was to share some of his embarrassingly obtained "goodie powder" with her, but after seeing that he barely had enough to get himself through the weekend, he was thankful that she hadn't been awake to accept the offer. He also realized that every self-degrading second he endured just to have this bag thrown on his lap was severely insulted by the weight of his reward in grams.

Karsyn shook his head with disappointment.

A small part of him wanted to backtrack to Ella's room and perpetrate every vile thought that crossed his mind. This urge - almost impossible to avoid now - intensified on the notion that he sacrificed his decency for the sake of her well being; therefore, his belief that she owed him in some form did increase.

His foot twisted in the direction of Ella's bedroom but he resisted turning himself completely.

He glimpsed down the end of the hallway.

Still, he didn't see one displaced shadow.

Silence remained uninterrupted.

He looked at the bag of powder again. Assuming there was only enough to cut a handful of lines, he went ahead and opened the door with his primary interest being to anesthetize himself close to insensibility.

Maybe he had watched her online content so much that she became too familiar for him to take any physical interest.

If he hadn't already encountered her and was just keeping the experience buried in the dismal abyss of self knowledge.

CHAPTER FIVE

At some point during the night the living room converted into a dark, quiet, and lifeless habitat. The kitchen and dining area were desolate as well. A blue light flashing on the kitchen microwave dispersed across the room and was the only source of visibility that prevented this stretch of space from succumbing to the billow of surrounding darkness. The dining quarters was entirely taken over by nightfall that also spread throughout the living room and extended to the top of the staircase. Outside of all the upstairs doors pulled shut, it was so dark that the hallway could be easily perceived as nonexistent.

While it should be suspected that life inside the Undergrove home was not consciously aware that the remaining hours of the night were slowly ticking away, there was a minor unspecified sound in the darkness upstairs which dismissed that theory.

Ella in her inebriated nirvana was completely incognizant of her door opening and then closing. Whoever disturbed the door was in her room at this point. The individual didn't seem to be in a hurry because they stood in the place they had stepped upon entering and admired Ella in her sultry state of rest. While their objective for prowling was unclear, it might be plausible to consider the purpose harbored something unethical based on the amount of time spent adoring her.

The uncalculated minutes spent gawking at her soon steered the individual to study the room. They recognized the computer was recording everything that would come to pass. Fortunately, they hadn't been caught in the frame since the camera pointed at the bed which was magnified onscreen to be the only area filmed. A more in depth observation of surroundings provided knowledge that the blinds on the window were open.

After familiarizing themself with their environment, the individual crossed the room and closed the monitor on the laptop to avoid recording anything that might happen. Then they approached the window and peeped outside through the slits in the blinds. They observed how much light was cast by the moon and also acknowledged the window was a good distance above ground level to prevent potential wanderers from eavesdropping. The mysterious visitor stepped away without shutting the blinds and approached the side of the bed.

As if every move was carefully orchestrated, the stranger picked up *Pinkie* from the bed and stashed it in the drawer of the nightstand before reaching inside the bottom of the lampshade and turning the light off. The room didn't become completely dark like the rest of the house since moonlight penetrated the blinds. Enough shine spread throughout the room and across Ella that the perpetrator didn't need additional light during the moment they might decide to perform their task.

The undetected guest lowered one hand onto her stomach and dragged it to her chest. They groped and pinched one breast aggressively. The rough treatment may have woke her under normal circumstances but it didn't phase her in this situation. The visitor rubbed across the other breast and abused it the same before gliding their hand back down on her stomach. Their fingers maneuvered past her belly button to rest along the elastic band of the panties snug around her waist. Of course, that hand didn't stay idle for too long. The individual pried their fingers between skin and elastic until the whole hand sank underneath Ella's panties. This wasn't an easy achievement but the strive could have been impossible if the shorts were not unfastened.

One fine characteristic the houseguest quickly discovered was that Ella shaved her pubic region. The skin was smooth and not one stubble of regrowth had been stumbled upon so far. She either shaved at some point in the past twenty-four hours or she got a Brazilian wax recently.

The visitant nudged one finger down the center of her vagina and the lips parted before closing and surrendering the finger to warm interior flesh. All that it took was a few gradual strokes from the clit to the opening before dry skin slickened to indicate that she was aroused while unconscious.

The individual withdrew their hand from inside the panties and brought it to her face, where they lowered the damp finger above the corner of her top lip and brushed sideways beneath her nose. Perhaps the reason for carrying out this move spawned from their desire to have Ella catch a whiff of her own cunt whenever she would awaken.

Following the gentle stride below her nose, the violator extended that same potentially foul finger and slid it inside her mouth. With the front of the finger pressing her tongue, the deviant raised their other hand to her chin and pushed until they felt her teeth graze their knuckle. Applying no lesser or greater amount of pressure, they graciously pulled the finger from her mouth while feeling it barely scrape teeth. Maybe the purpose of being inside her mouth involved wanting Ella to taste herself whenever she would awaken.

What the intruder did next was unbuckle their belt from their pants and then remove it. The stranger reached under her head and wrapped the buckle side of the belt halfway around her throat before pulling the opposite end through the buckle and latching one of the notches to constrict the leather against her neck, but not too tight that it might fatally strangle her. In fact, the perpetrator tugged once on the strap to make sure there was plenty of slack between her and the buckle before laying it straight down her body, and then let go when it came to an end just a few inches away from touching her belly button.

The dusky figure crept around the foot of the bed and turned toward her like some malignant paranormal entity surveying its host. The individual didn't waste a lot of time inspecting her because an influx of anxiousness evidently got the best of them when they leaned forward and curled both arms under the back of her knees. Ella was jolted to the edge of the bed, and the aggressor didn't cease until her legs were removed enough to have her feet touch the floor.

Pushing her thighs together and potentially simplifying the hassle in whatever came next, the prowler curled their fingers inside her denim shorts and pulled them down along with her bright yellow panties. Those eager hands wrestled the clothes past her knees before the deviant squatted and continued sliding them to her feet.

With a predictably unethical scheme in mind, the exploiter spread her legs and relocated themself in the gap between them. They grabbed one of her thighs with one hand and the belt with the other. Then they coiled the leather around their hand until they considered the hold solid enough to pull themself to her midsection.

Her genuinely engaging taste was the culprit behind the violator tugging the belt without providing the excessively overbearing strength to disrupt her sleep. In reality, they could toss her around like some rag doll and she would not be disturbed.

Their tongue stretched the width of one lip and then spanned across the other. Saliva mixed with the secretion of vaginal sweat spread to both thighs. The predator felt and smelled Ella's messy discharge smear around their mouth. They dipped their tongue onto the outside of her tiny opening and licked all around it while their nose buried against the clit and succumbed to getting plastered by the cocktail of shared bodily fluids.

Presumably satisfied with the outcome of eating her out, the prowler unwrapped the belt from their hand and stood in front of her.

They unfastened their pants.

And then they did what was undoubtedly their intent from the start.

They dropped their pants along with their boxers and revealed an erection eager to invade her. Unquestionably a male perpetrator, he reached under her legs and dragged her toward him until her ass sagged over the side of the bed.

Then he stroked his cock a few times as a means to preserve its solidity before grappling her legs and placing the back of her feet against his shoulders.

The ultimate question remained.

Who was responsible for the non consensual treatment of Ella Pearson?

Did Cody honestly develop a hunger by watching her sexualized behavior that he had no control over the irresistible desire to try her for himself? Or could it be that Karsyn was at his wits end of fantasizing and finally reacted to the unavoidable urge and began taking vengeance out on her for what happened to him earlier?

There was Jake also.

The criminal drug trafficker did articulate his interest in wanting a piece of her. Was it possible that he returned to the property under the assumption that everyone was asleep and broke in somehow before locating the correct room without disturbing the others?

Three prominent suspects.

Just one of them proved malign in their heart enough to assault someone not in the condition to retaliate.

His ruthless pursuit intensified and left nothing to the imagination when he stepped forward and lunged his dick inside her - ramming himself against the back of her thighs and grunting because the motion was quick and aggressive. Perhaps the reason for giving such a violent thrust involved the ideology that delivering profound treatment would allow Ella to sense her unwarranted abuse in the depth of unconsciousness. While it was plausible that she didn't feel anything inflicted on her during the assault, he pulled back but then quickly slammed against her again. The force jolted her entire body and shook the mattress; however, she remained unresponsive to his hostility.

If living out his sadistic fantasy was a predetermined aspiration, then it might be chilling to predict the severity of how far he could be willing to go to factualize events.

Leaning forward and driving her knees toward her chest, he got into the rhythm of grinding back and forth swiftly. The repetitive technique was flawless in the sense that he must have spent multiple nights materializing this particular scenario in his thoughts. Each time that he pulled away, his dick almost tore free and definitely would have if he didn't stop in time just for the head to plug her opening. Every time that he shoved forward, he sank up to his nuts in slick warmth while her and the bed continued to jerk. On occasion, he plowed against her in a particular way that caused the bed to squeak, and he probably wasn't impressed about creating this anguished melody because he was trying everything in his ability to stay quiet.

He gasped almost constantly.

Groaned every once in a while.

But he did these things in a subtle way not to involve too much noise.

Since her legs were propped against his shoulders to secure her position, he let go of her thighs only to reach down and grab her chest. He fondled her breasts like a degenerate scum would do; displaced their position while squeezing them without a care for their level of sensitivity, and pierced the nipples with a pinch so hard that it could have potentially roused her to scream with enhanced pain if she was awake.

He withdrew from one breast and extended his hand to her face before using two fingers as hooks to pry into her mouth and seperate the jaws. Keeping his fingers in her mouth and admiring the peacefully balanced lack of expression, he paused from making further movement and reveled in the feeling of a marinated orgasm swarm his tempered flesh after thrusting even deeper. Secretion wasn't only felt; he smelled its unsavory fragrance.

Taking his fingers out of her mouth while pulling away from her breast at the same time, he grasped the end of the belt laying on her stomach before rearing upright and grabbing the calve behind one of her legs. He drifted away from pressing the back of her legs, but then he suddenly jerked forward and rammed against them again. He soon got his feisty rhythm back and with it came the plashing sound associated with jabbing her sufficiently lubricated inside.

Ella's shoulders raised off the bed and her head tipped backwards when he yanked the strap and held it steady in front of her legs. He scraped his fingers up her thigh and grunted twice before his thrusts stopped just to have him squirm while mashed against her. A moderate tingle scaled throughout his legs which indicated how close he was to achieving satisfaction, but he focused on Ella more than his sense of elation and this concentration seemed to help delay the probable result.

Her shoulders elevated higher off the bed and her head slumped backwards as far as it could go when he pulled the belt close to him. He could have probably yanked her upright but didn't; instead, he kept her strangely suspended like some abominable ornament representing a sexual crucifixion. Aware that he was very close to ejaculating, he reinstated giving it to her ferociously.

The bed frame smacked the wall.

The perpetrator groaned and growled.

He seemed unbothered about not subduing the noise like he practiced earlier.

When the inescapable yet desirous moment struck, he pressed against Ella and stalled from making any further movement as his testicular fluid burst inside her. Rotating each shoulder separately after he came in her caused Ella's legs to drop from his shoulders and her feet plummet onto the floor.

He stepped back but didn't let go of the belt. He actually tugged the strap as he moved backwards and didn't quit until she was sitting upright. He reached underneath her chin, raised her head, and adored the good as dead demeanor before leaning down and giving her a quick peck on the lips.

What the vile assailant did next might honestly be worse than the initial abuse. He reached between her legs and ground his fingers against her vagina, swiping upwards and lubricating them with his and her sticky discharge. Then he raised his hand to her face and brushed the tainted fingertips across her lips before slipping them into her mouth to scrub the syrupy blend of bodily fluids on her tongue. He left her mouth and lowered his hand onto the buckle fastened around her throat. Still holding the loose end with the other hand, he wrapped the strap around it before bringing it up to assist with unfastening the buckle.

Instead of carefully guiding her back onto the bed, he carelessly allowed her incognizance to drop her on the mattress.

Physically desecrated...

A living sex doll that was no longer deemed an asset.

The man bent down and pulled up his pants. He fastened his jeans before hurrying the belt through the loops and clamping the buckle. Then he stepped back and away from the bed, showing another level of indecency by leaving Ella laying with shorts and panties around her ankles and the shirt raised above her breasts.

He took one long hard look at her while walking backwards slowly toward the door. Perhaps he imagined how events might soon unfold in the hours ahead; Ella waking to shockingly discover the tangy flavor of genital juice in its slimy texture spread throughout her mouth, and the aftermath of indulgence leaking out of her cunt long after his departure.

He obviously wanted her to be aware that she had been assaulted.

Emotionally mortify her into accepting the credence that if she was going to strut around, portraying herself to be a whore, then she was going to get used and demoralized as one.

CHAPTER SIX

The bed squealed when jarred.

Blair opened her eyes to the view of darkness all around. Her first thought was that Cody just now got in bed, but then she wasn't one-hundred percent positive because she didn't know how long she'd been asleep. She honestly didn't know what time it was; therefore, she couldn't predict if she had been sleeping for two hours or if it had been only thirty minutes.

Uncertainty was definitely a common theme in the Undergrove home.

She wished that Cody slept with his arms around her. Honestly, she couldn't remember the last time they cuddled. She wasn't able to recall how long it had been since he showed her any genuine passion. Whenever he kissed her, she didn't feel a connection to him. His effort always seemed to be forced. Sadly, she also believed that he didn't spend enough time faking it.

Despite having an unborn child, Blair sensed that she was alone in the relationship because Cody didn't commit himself in the marital aspect. Those in-depth husband and wife conversations that she used to enjoy had gone nonexistent for over a year. Small talk was pretty much all they shared at this point. When they did interact, he was never fully involved. Either he zoned out watching television or he diverted his attention to whatever was on his phone. Didn't matter which of the two was more common; they both bore an equal injustice by denying her to have his attention.

She didn't quite understand why she should lay there and get herself worked up over failed efforts to communicate, because experience proved how he was a know-it-all and intentional smartass with his replies. Realistically, they probably got along better now than how they might if he did speak often.

Keeping one hand tucked under the pillow, she reached under the blanket and rested the other against the bulge of her stomach. Her instant thought was that she was dealing with this pregnancy in the sense of being a single parent. Cody never spent one minute of downtime to pet her belly. She didn't recall there ever being a moment when he asked her if she was okay, and he certainly never bragged about looking forward to raising a child together.

She wasn't accustomed to receiving this type of cold treatment. She remembered how Ella's father pampered and tended to her needs throughout the pregnancy. She even recollected how he went above and beyond his expectations after Ella was born. Never once did she have to ask for anything because he was always one step ahead.

Cody and Ella's father were definitely not alike. The extent of their dissimilarities was something she didn't know for the longest time, because Cody had mastered hiding his true colors during the dating phase.

She rolled onto her back. It wasn't easy to readjust with another life developing inside. In fact, it literally drained every bit of energy just to get situated.

She peered into darkness on his side of the bed and contemplated how badly she wanted to twist and throw her arm across his side, but she refrained from doing what she wished he would do because she was tired of having to instigate affection and communication between them. Everything lacking in their marriage eventually instilled her with a lonesome feeling that took on a physical property.

Cody felt her move next to him. Unknown to Blair, he was awake and hadn't slept. Keeping to himself, he had nothing against comforting her but it wasn't in his nature to offer support in all of its forms. This was the main reason why he and Karsyn's mother didn't stay together. He just wasn't equipped to provide a partner with genuine affection.

Another element of disaster that strained their marriage was Blair's excessive need for reassurance. Her constant demand to know if he loved her went on for what he believed was five months straight. He often found himself forced to coddle her insecurities - always having to address his love by showing ridiculous amounts of simulated devotion. His best efforts got criticized for not being adequate and eventually drove him away.

And then there was Ella.

Eccentric, boisterous, and glimmering with habitual positivity. Physical characteristics, luridly similar to her mother, Ella was a more athletically built and ravishing version of Blair. Although she dyed her hair black in order not to be her mother's clone, this drastic change actually enhanced her natural beauty and was the perfect tint for accompanying her pale complexion. Magnified the beam in those blue eyes also.

He was aware of how strict he was on her and it was a decision that he didn't plan to change. His reason for treating her sternly resulted from the sadist trait in his Machiavellian personality, which he was knowledgeable about possessing. In his dark triad of beliefs, Ella wasn't just a stepdaughter - she was also a personal belonging. He felt more compelled to manage her every move than he did about controlling Blair.

What didn't help Ella was the fact that he invaded a very private aspect of her life. Then again, the argument might exist that privacy was irrelevant when it came to her intentionally promoting her vulnerabilities for the world to see. Despite the validity of public access, this situation involving him and Ella was blatantly immoral. He acknowledged the distastefulness in viewing her X-rated material but he couldn't deny himself the enjoyment, because he became addicted not just to seeing her nude but also to witnessing how far she was willing to go to publicize herself sexually. His profound infatuation with her turned corrupt when his perception shifted to only view her as a filthy, cock crazed slut.

He shut his eyes and saw Ella. Duplicates of her, actually. The sight reminded him of the Brady Bunch cast in their individual blocks, multiplied by ten. No version of her appeared the same. Some images exposed her wearing a bra and panties. Other displays were less revealing by showing her in a bra and denim shorts. But then, there were also those particular visuals that concealed nothing and broadcast her in the buff.

He fought to clear his mind, but too many visits to

her online portfolio had stained his thoughts.

It seemed that Ella engraved herself as a permanent fixture.

His fascination with her never failed to stir excitement, and the standard currently applied beneath the blanket in defiance of him not wanting the experience.

Blair looked at the ceiling overshadowed in the night. Elevated hormones had her longing to be held but she remained resilient by not rolling over and slinging her arm around him. The pregnancy caused her to feel and think things that she didn't normally endure. Depression in lonesomeness had her believing she was abandoned; something that an expecting mother shouldn't have to sustain.

On top of her sense of seclusion, Blair felt unattractive. Stomach sagging over her waist, puffy cheeks caused by water water retention, acne, and always having to blow her nose into a tissue; she was absolutely appalled by herself. Such negativity regarding her appearance persuaded her that Cody acted the way he did because he was disgusted.

All of these inhospitable feelings were a new experience for her. She didn't really know how to cope. Things were completely different than when she was pregnant with Ella. Thinking back to that particular period in her life, she could hardly fathom that she was barely in her twenties when she conceived. Twenty-one years and four months old, to be exact. Back then, she was more slender, tight bodied, and wrinkle free. Getting pregnant didn't have much of an effect on her and the symptoms associated were relatively mild.

Thinking about Ella, she did somewhat agree with Cody's impression that her and Ella shared similarities, but she didn't consider the twin resemblance since there was a significant age gap. She actually thought that Ella might be slightly more beautiful than what she was at that age. One thing she could not ignore was the attractiveness, because Cody made it apparent without stating the fact. He made it obvious by doing what he thought was him sneakily checking her out. Ella seemed to never catch him gawking, but Blair noticed on multiple occasions. She didn't pay much attention to Karsyn, but it wouldn't alarm her if he reacted the same since he was his father's son.

She didn't place all the blame on Cody for creating so many uncomfortable situations. She cast equal responsibility on Ella for instigating matters. The way she would prance throughout the house in shorts riding up her crotch and shirts that sometimes showed her nipples protruding when she wasn't wearing a bra. Furthermore, she firmly believed that Ella was aware of her questionable behavior.

The circumstance was becoming more frequent and Blair sensed the undesirable increase of jealousy within herself recently. She didn't favor the idea of comparing her daughter as a rival because she upheld sense enough to understand that Ella dressed and acted how she did since she was a young lady, still on the path to self discovery. She also didn't believe that Cody, regardless of his malevolent attributes, would act impulsively on whatever spur of the moment idea that might cross his morally deteriorating mind.

Jealousy, anger, envy - all were traits of the human

condition that she could not prevent herself from suffering. She told herself a thousand times already that such crazed thinking was going to drive her mad, but this recognition never once helped mitigate the turmoil.

She turned away from Cody.

Struggled effortlessly to find a margin of calmness beneath chaos screaming inside her head. She felt that she could scream aloud and Cody still would not comfort her. Or have the decency to assure her that everything was going to be okay.

Praying for eventual sleep to stray her from this dismally cloistered purgatory, Blair rubbed her belly and wept silently in the absence of their consolidation.

Both of them lay awake in singular worlds.

One and the other, existing differently in opposing mindsets.

dition that she could not prevent herself in a suffering she will herself a thousand times already that such magical thinking was going to drive her mad, but this recognition never once helped.

She turned away from Cody.

Sunrise effortlessly of India tumult of calmness beneath those screaming inside her head. She felt that she mentally closed p

CHAPTER SEVEN

Neon light flashing on the microwave directed an unspecified occupant in their voyage across the kitchen. They made their way around quite well without the need for stable light to guide them. The area of interest was below the countertop next to the sink.

One shadowy hand extended to grasp the drawer handle and pull slowly. While it was likely their intent not to create a stir, metal objects striking each other did pitch a sudden disturbance that was relatively loud given the eerie silence accompanying the early hour. The disruption was temporary since the individual slid the drawer out halfway before stopping and peering down at its contents only visible during each rapid cast of dull visibility. What seemed to catch and hold their attention was the bundle of large utensils on the right. They reached inside and fumbled through these particular items. The individual pulled back after sifting beneath the top layer and closed the drawer before raising the chosen object in front of them. The display caught in the on and off again neon glow was a stainless steel grill fork. This prowler must have been satisfied with its sharpness after touching the two pointed tips because they kept the utensil in their possession when turning and stepping away from the counter.

The individual proceeded past the microwave,

where the clock blinked twelve 'o' clock as if the power had been knocked out at some point and the time never reset once electricity was restored. They entered the living room which greeted them with pure darkness but somehow managed to cross the room and not make contact with any furniture sitting in close proximity.

The fact that this person was capable of passing without incident was odd. How did they know the layout of the house so well?

Could this be the same deviant that violated Ella, and why were they now weaponizing themself?

What sinister agenda was actually at play?

The ultimate uncertainty remained.

If Karsyn or Cody had been responsible for the assault, then might it be one of them prepared to silence her from going public after she discovered what occurred?

The person was too knowledgeable about the layout and seemed strangely educated in knowing how to ascend the stairs without causing them to squeak. Interestingly, creaks in the staircase was exactly what Karsyn listened for earlier. The assailant emerged upon the threshold of the most obscure part of the house and went ahead into its depth. Each gradual progression brought them closer to an apparent act of ill intent while staying to the right side and brushing their fingers along the wall. Suddenly, their hand collided with a round metal object after trekking just a brief distance.

A knob.

The individual stopped, gripped the handle, and turned toward the door hidden by darkness.

They twisted the knob.

Pushed slowly.

The door opened and what was revealed in the ongoing lackluster glow of moonlight launched through the bedroom window was Ella's indecently exposed body laying on the foot of the bed. She remained in the same position she had been left following the assault; consequently, it was indisputable that she hadn't woken to find out the unsettling misconduct performed on her. If she would have known her predicament, then it might be logical to presume the anonymous guest would not be lurking because everyone in the home would be out of bed and surely aghast by the commotion of her screaming and crying.

Unfortunately, nothing about the latter pertained to the situation.

The fork wielding visitant stepped inside the room and shut the door. They approached the bed cautiously. Perhaps they weren't sure if she might wake to the slightest sound. But she didn't awaken; she didn't stir at all.

The fork lowered and its two long tines pressed the side of her face before dragging gently underneath her chin without scratching. The stranger glided the teeth down her neck and along her chest before leading them on top of one breast. One of the tines scraped the nipple since there was a sizable gap between it and the other one, but not enough pressure was applied to scratch the surface. The sharp tip pressed the nipple for just a short while longer before both tines moved slowly upon her stomach. Stainless steel clawed the skin but then ceased abruptly and bore down against flesh on either side of the belly button.

The houseguest eased around the foot of the bed,

and still didn't react as if alarmed to find her oddly situated with her genitals exposed. The likelihood that this same person was also responsible for defiling her could only increase based on their preternatural behavior.

The fork dragged below her stomach and was angled in a way that its tips pressed firmly against her skin. The tines scraped and did not stop until they poked the grimy exterior between her legs. The guest gave it a quick push in an attempt to instigate a reaction but was probably astounded when discovering that she didn't entertain what was anticipated. Those spiked tips withdrew from applying pressure after it became obvious that Ella was incapable of conveying discomfort.

It might be reasonable to assume that the aggressor would pull back since she didn't satisfy their intent to issue agitation, but they didn't retreat. Instead, they slid the fork from her vagina and relocated on her stomach; however, this time the tines brushed along her side rather than jab the scrawny flesh on the sides of her belly button.

The intruder checked for an expression but still did not recognize a hint of negatively induced excitement.

All of a sudden, the fork raised from her body before the wretched hand swooped down and attacked by savagely burying half the length of the tines in the side of her stomach. Blood elevated outside the pair of wounds and pooled briefly before cascading down her side and staining the bed. One quick tug and the attacker ripped those stainless steel teeth from her body. The tines weren't quite stainless anymore since they were coated with her life fluid dripping from the tips. Having nothing wedged to slow the flow brought about severe bleeding. In a matter of seconds the stain enlarged alongside her hip while not yet absorbed through the sheet and into the mattress.

The harmful intruder didn't spend too long admiring their grisly achievement, because the giant meat fork sped down again and dug into her stomach; directly beneath her navel. The merciless ravager twisted the handle for the reason to lengthen the wounds larger than the width of the spikes, still implanted. This callous act was a definite representation of the criminal desire to inflict trauma based purely on passion rather than some momentary thrill.

Almost double the amount of blood spilled out of these new wounds due to the additional cruel treatment. Streams of bodily fluid ran together and painted her pussy before dripping beneath her crotch and forming a puddle identical to the one beside her.

The attacker yanked the fork from her body and then raised it almost above their head before swinging down and striking Ella for the third time. The teeth sank deep inside the lower region of her stomach and didn't strike far from where the prior injury. Fresh blood spilled and blended with fluid still pouring out of the recent wound before gushing between her legs and widening the stain beneath her so much that crimson streaked the portion of blanket hanging over the foot of the bed.

The aggressor retrieved the weapon and adored her bleeding out excessively. The severity of blood spilled was ghastly enough to raise the belief that she had been struck approximately a dozen times. Of course, alcohol in her system, which thinned her blood, did not help to discredit this visual misrepresentation.

The assailant apparently got tired of standing back

and marveling at their horrid artistry because they lunged unexpectedly...

Stabbed.

Withdrew-

Stabbed.

Withdrew-

STABBED!

Ella's lower midsection became the pictorialization of cold blooded homicide, and the bed was so messily decorated that whatever degree of life she might be clinging onto would be surprising.

The perpetrator stripped the tines from her flesh and walked around to the side of the bed. They stopped halfway and stood next to her. The devient reached down and swiped one hand through her dark hair to show they possessed a margin of affection amongst their rage. After adoring her with a temporary loving sentiment, they turned her head in the opposite direction and skimmed their fingers along her neck before vacating once their fingers grazed her collarbone.

There seemed to be a moment of bizarre nothingness between Ella and her murderer.

The aggressor just stood alongside the bed and analyzed Ella's ongoing failure to show expression while the essence of life flowed out of her. Maybe this individual was closely observing to try and spot any potential sign of life.

If Ella was alive or dead, it really didn't matter.

The fork came down and speared her in the throat. One of its tines may have severed the carotid artery because blood erupted instantly and splattered a messy trail across the side of the bed. Ella may have possibly survived prior injuries but this one certainly gave a fatal impression. Perhaps the aggressor believed this last strike finished the job because what unusual event transpired was them reaching down and peeling open her closest eyelid. Indeed, the reason for this odd spectacle was known only to the morbid invader. The eyeball rolled around, even aimed at the attacker a few times, but Ella didn't react. They let go of her eyelid, believing the reason it moved irregularly was due to her being in a deep state of REM sleep. Then again, she had received more torment than what her body should be able to handle; so, the cause was reconsidered and then assumed that her sporadic eye movement was the outcome of distressed nerves responding to gradual organ failure.

Although it was within reason to suspect that she had succumbed to her injuries, her attacker doubled down on diminishing whatever slim chance of survival by driving the fork into her neck another time. Its long teeth penetrated the center of her throat. Satisfied with the amount of blood shed in what was now one sadistically brutal crime scene, the intruder pulled the fork from her flesh and lowered it at their side.

Ella showed no backlash toward the aftermath.

She didn't spasm.

Didn't open her eyes.

Didn't make a sound.

It seemed the ramification prompted a satisfying conclusion.

Which involved putting Ella Pearson in a predicament where events pertaining to the entire night would remain perpetually silent.

Forever questionable.

CHAPTER EIGHT

"911... What is your emergency?"

Breathing, low volume crying, and an inaudible whisper was the response from darkness.

"911... Again, what is your emergency?"

"Help," the quiet voice stated with difficulty.

"Ma'am, I'm having a hard time hearing you. What's going on?"

Suddenly, there was light. A messy smear ran down the cover of the electrical box and also sampled the wall with a grisly makeover before the bloody hand that was responsible drew away. Then came the sound of the door shutting quietly.

"Ma'am, are you still with me?"

Silence followed the operator's inquiry on both ends of the line.

"Ma'am, if you're there... Speak to me. I'm not able to assist without you giving me pertinent information. Okay?"

Blair stepped forward and was instantly petrified by her reflection. Shock broadened her eyes while she stared at herself trembling in the mirror. Both of her hands were covered with blood with no other part of her stained. She didn't appear to have any self injuries that would explain the situation.

She sniffled quietly and then attempted to state her claim. "I need the police. An ambulance. Somebody. My daughter's been killed."

Admitting Ella's death caused her to cry to the point of almost losing control. She raised her forearm and swiped across her face because she didn't want to spread blood that was thick on her hands. In fact, she was surprised that she hadn't dropped the phone since it did nearly slide from her grip a few times.

Trying to gather herself when things seemed to be happening too fast, she continued. "I tried waking her but she didn't answer, and I- I don't know. There's blood everywhere."

"You said that your daughter is unresponsive, correct?"

"Yes," she gasped.

"Do you know what happened? I need as much information as possible to pass on to the authorities. That way they'll be better equipped to handle the situation when they get there."

Blair turned the cold water on, smearing blood all around the knob. "I think my husband killed her. I don't know how. He's been obsessed with her for a long time."

"Where is your husband right now?"

"He's in bed. I'm trying to be quiet so that I don't wake him and he comes after me."

"What is his name?"

"Cody... Cody Undergrove."

"Thank you, Blair. Now is there anyone else in the home?"

"Yeah. My stepson. He's the only other person here,

besides my daughter."

"*His name?*"

"Karsyn."

"*Karsyn Undergrove?*"

"Yes," she answered swiftly.

"*And where is he?*"

"I think he's in bed too. I don't know for sure. I haven't seen him."

"*Okay. Now let's get back to your daughter. What is her name, and how old is she?*"

"She's nineteen." Blair rinsed blood off one hand and then switched holding the phone to cleanse the other. Of course, washing her hands didn't keep them clear from recollecting blood since it was on the phone as well. "Her name's Ella."

"*Okay. Can you give me your address, Blair?*"

"395 River Rock Drive-"

"*In Pembroke. Is that correct?*"

"Yeah. That's right." She turned the water off which further recontaminated her hand due to the soiled handle. "We're the fifth house on the right."

"*I've passed the information on. There are officers in the area and they should be there soon. Is there any place safe enough for you to wait until they arrive?*"

"I'm not sure," Blair sobbed. "I mean, I can stay here in the room but that isn't going to stop anyone from getting to me if they wanted."

"*I understand. I'm just trying to look out for your best interest until the police show up.*"

"Please, hurry. I don't know when he's going to get

up," she begged.

"They are in pursuit and will be there as fast as they can. Is the door unlocked for them to get in?"

"I don't think so. Everyone was in bed."

"Alright. I'm going to need you to unlock the door. Can you do that for me?"

She dabbed her eyes with the back of her hand. "It's downstairs… So, it'll take me a bit to get there. I'm pregnant."

"I understand. But I need you to do this, okay?"

She took a deep breath and sighed. "Okay."

"Remain calm and quiet. Everything is going to be okay. They're not far."

"Should I step outside?" she asked.

"No. Do not walk out of the house. I don't want you doing anything that will have the police not knowing what to expect."

"Okay. I'm getting ready to go downstairs." She turned the light off and the room got so dark that she couldn't see the mirror in front of her. Tilting the phone away from her face, she used the light on its screen to help her locate the knob. "Are they here yet?"

"They're on the way. They should be there any moment now. Just stay calm and do everything I've told you."

Blair opened the door and confronted the expanse of darkness awaiting her emergence. She poked her head through the doorway and checked both directions. No light beamed from either side. She tiptoed forward and turned to the right. Light from the phone didn't reach the floor but she had roamed the hallway so many times that she could navigate it with her eyes closed.

"Blair, are you still with me?"

Although the dispatcher's voice didn't blast through the phone, Blair still cringed at the thought of someone else in the house hearing the voice. Not disturbing Cody was her primary concern, but she also didn't want Karsyn taking notice and storming out of his room because he'd certainly stir a commotion that would awaken his father.

"I'm here," she whispered in her quietest voice.

"Are you downstairs?"

She wanted to tell the operator to shut the hell up but she refrained from speaking what was on her mind because she understood the woman was just doing her job. She reacted by not saying anything instead.

Blair stopped and turned in the direction of where she believed the staircase descended. Having faith that the handrail was within reach without taking another step, she extended her hand and waded through darkness until she smacked the side of the banister. She grabbed it immediately, and kind of pulled herself down the first few steps.

"Blair, I need you to talk to me so that I know you're okay."

"I'm going," she finally replied.

"One of the officer's has informed me that he's almost at your residence. I want you to tell me when you see him."

"I'm not at the door yet," she stated quietly.

"Okay. Let me know when you've reached the door and unlocked it so that I can relay the information to officers."

Blair felt like it took forever to reach the halfway point since she wasn't quick on her feet. Not knowing where to step didn't help her progress either. She basically scooted the bottom of her feet from one step to the next in fear of stumbling forward. Moving closer to ground level, she felt anticipation-

Crek.

"Shit," she griped.

"What's wrong?"

"Nothing," Blair whispered.

She hesitated after the stair squalled and listened for even the most vague sound to spill through the opening behind her. Fortunately, she didn't pick up on any noise following the one she caused accidentally.

Blair proceeded once more.

"Don't be alarmed if you do not hear sirens. They have them turned off for your safety. Their emergency lights will be flashing but no sirens. Okay?"

"Okay," she uttered.

Her feet touched what felt like a wide range of level flooring and she automatically assumed that she clearned the staircase. Despite not being able to see her surroundings, Blair had seen the layout of the room so much that she practically memorized the door was about four steps ahead of the stairs. She reached out and swiped the air while advancing. As expected, she made contact with the door after a few more steps. Unsurprisingly, the knob wasn't the first thing she went for; instead, she swatted her hand up the wall beside the door and the room filled with light after she struck the lightswitch. She squinted instantly while her eyes struggled to adjust.

"I'm at the door," she mentioned, before turning and eyeing the top of the stairs.

The path remained clear.

"You're doing good, Blair. Can you see if any officers have arrived? You should be able to see their flashers when they get there."

She stepped alongside the full size window next to the door and pulled its curtain back slightly. Peering down the dark street that crossed in front of the house, Blair didn't recognize any sign of police presence.

"No. I don't see anyone. I can't see anything actually," she responded.

"Okay. Well... I've been advised there are officers in your vicinity. There will be a heavy presence based on the nature of your call; so, don't panic."

She continued to hold the curtain back and stare out into the valley of darkness. She eventually did notice the rotation of dull blue light spinning off the house across the street. That same circulating light bounced quickly from the home and stretched across the lawn in front of it before drifting onto the road.

Blair unlocked the door.

"They're here," she mumbled promptly.

"Stay on the line with me until they are inside the house with you."

Her speculation was solidified when one, two-

Five...

Nine police cars arrived on the scene. They didn't park in any particular alignment. In fact, it appeared they stalled abruptly and blocked the road from passage. The far reaching glow of spinning blue light lit up the lawn.

Policemen didn't hesitate to exit their vehicles. Some kept their distance to serve as backup for the remaining few that approached the house with their hands on their weapons in the event of having to pull a quick draw.

Blair let go of the curtain and went for the knob. She opened the door and was greeted instantly by several officers that didn't speak a word when entering the home. They walked past her and spread throughout the living room.

"They're inside," she mentioned to the operator.

"Okay, Blair. You can hang up the phone now."

The dispatcher ended the call before she had time to lower the phone.

"Blair Undergrove?" asked one of the older officers, staring at her while crossing the doorway.

"Umm... Yeah," she answered, seemingly beside herself in all the commotion.

He glanced at the staircase and pointed toward the top. "I assume that's where the bedrooms are?"

She nodded when replying. "Yes."

The officer pulled the gun from his belt and clicked the safety off before holding it down beside him. "I'm Detective Roismann. I'm in charge of the investigation. Correct me if I'm wrong, but you stated to dispatch that your husband may have wounded your daughter, right?"

"Yes, sir."

"And where is he now?"

"In bed."

"Asleep?" Detective Roismann inquired.

She shrugged before wiping away. "I think so. He was the last time I saw him."

"There is someone else in the house too, correct?"

She nodded again. "My stepson, yes."

"They're all upstairs?"

"Yes, sir."

"Okay." Detective Roismann looked at the officer standing idle in front of the couch and signaled for him to approach. "Blair, this is Officer Ryve. He is going to sit with you while we go upstairs and evaluate the situation. I will have more questions for you after we wrap up our initial observations."

"All right." She stepped away from the door and crept in the direction of Officer Ryve as he walked toward her also. "Is there anything you need me to do right now?"

Detective Roismann motioned for several of his fellow officers to proceed ahead of him. "No, ma'am. The only thing I want from you is to sit in the living room and wait for me to come back like I previously stated."

"Oh. Okay," she said, before Officer Ryve grabbed her arm gently and walked with her to the couch.

Four officers led the way upstairs and Detective Roismann followed closely behind while the remaining three trailed him. Not many steps squalled during their pursuit but having eight men go up them at once did kind of balance out the pressure applied to the structure. The lead officer made it to the top, and when on the verge of turning the corner leading into darkness, he reached on the wall alongside the stairs and flipped the lightswitch. The hallway brightened and light cast onto the policemen stalled on the steps.

Blair was still able to see their progress since they hadn't advanced further. She hoped that Karsyn didn't awaken and come barreling out of his room to get himself wedged in the center of what could turn into a hostile situation. She also prayed that Cody would not storm out of their bedroom and cause a confrontation that might result in having nine guns getting drawn on him. Keeping a firm gaze on the top of the stairs, she watched each policeman disappear gradually into the hallway.

"Psst," Detective Roismann sounded out quietly.

The three officers in front of him stopped and turned to find out what was in his plans for their next move. Detective Roismann spent a moment examining the layout ahead. He recognized that a door on the left and another directly across from it was closest to them. Then he glimpsed at the last two doors, seeing one of them on the left and the last one facing them from the end of the hallway.

He directed two of his men to take position at the nearest door on the left. One man moved against the wall next to the right side and the second one positioned himself on the left. Both men raised their weapons as if prepared for an ambush. Roismann implemented a form of sign language to signal the other two officers to take the same position at the door on the right. He turned to the policemen behind him and gestured for them to keep watch on the remaining doors without actually sending them to scamper to the end of the hall.

Roismann raised his own weapon and aimed forward when grabbing the handle of the left side door. He took a deep anxious breath while uncertain about what awaited them.

He turned the knob.

Glanced at both men and noticed they seemed just as tense as him.

Then he opened the door.

Silent darkness met him from the other side.

Detective Roismann kept his gun positioned since he wasn't aware of what potential dangers might exist ahead. He reached inside the room and fumbled his fingers along the wall until striking the lightswitch. The room brightened to show the situation in front of him involved no altercation whatsoever. Roismann and the two deputies peered into the empty bathroom. Nothing appeared to be out of the ordinary but Roismann did make note of blood on a faucet handle. He remembered seeing specks of blood on Blair's hands and so he didn't dwell too much on this strand of evidence since he related it with her. He'd been a detective for thirty-two years; therefore, he had seen and experienced a lot in the span of his career. After a while, he discovered that the most obvious piece of evidence didn't always tie to malicious matters.

"I'll bring this up to her but I think it's irrelevant," he mentioned to the officers nearest him.

Roismann gave the room one last look over but still didn't see any incriminating evidence. He turned his back to the room and glanced at the policemen across from him before approaching the second door. He gripped his gun more firmly and hugged the trigger. With one room exposed, Roismann knew that his chance of entering into a confrontation had improved. He didn't reach for the knob until the two officers behind him took their position.

When he opened the door, Roismann was welcomed by the same darkness that greeted him upon discovering the bathroom. Another similarity was the fact that they'd not got ambushed. Blair did inform him that Cody was sleeping to the best of her knowledge; but still, he was prepared for the possibility that Cody was anticipating their arrival.

Detective Roismann turned the light on inside the room and was appalled by the presentation. Not even the information provided to him by dispatch had given him any thought in comparison to the scene laid out before him. The young woman sprawled out on the lower half of the bed was inappropriately displayed with almost half her body bloodstained. Roismann bowed his head with sympathy for what the victim must have endured during her final moments. He didn't speak his thoughts to his fellow officers but he believed they too suspected that she was caddishly assaulted prior to being slain. At no point did he feel the need to enter the room and check Ella for a pulse because the sense of homicide was eerily heavy in the atmosphere. In all of his experience he never got used to the feelings of filth and sorrow that were associated.

"Let's get this sonuvabitch," he told his men.

Before they got a chance to advance all together, Detective Roismann pointed toward her horribly ravaged body and then looked at each officer standing behind either side of him.

"You two get in there and comb every inch of the area. I want every fine detail analyzed. Starting right now, no one crosses this doorway without my authorization," he stated.

"Yes, sir," one of the officers replied quickly, and he and his partner hustled into the bedroom.

Roismann turned to the officers that had served as

his backup when they all arrived at the bathroom. "Devan, I want you to get in touch with dispatch and have them send forensics down here on the double. We've got an atrocity on our hands and I don't want us dicking around any longer than necessary."

"Sure thing," Devan said.

Detective Roismann looked at the second officer and pointed at the last door on the left. "Eyes on that door with your weapon raised and ready to strike at any time. If it opens so much as a crack, I want you prepared for the worst case scenario."

"Yes, sir," said the officer, aiming his gun as directed.

Roismann acknowledged the final three officers awaiting his command. "Let's move."

All four men walked to the door at the end of the hall. Of course, Detective Roismann led this entourage since decades of experience made him better equipped to handle the unexpected. Opening the door introduced them to whatever uncertainty dwelling in the dark. Roismann glanced over either shoulder to make sure that his men were prepared before he reached inside the unknown and turned the light on.

They didn't stumble into an aggressive confrontation like expected but did find themselves within reach of anything becoming possible. Detective Roismann pointed his weapon with intent to use it at any moment while his unit dispersed inside the room. One officer dashed around the far side of the bed. Another one moved to the foot of it. The third policeman bolted to the nearest side. Four weapons with four fingers snug against their triggers aimed at Cody, sleeping. The blanket was pulled up to his neck and so neither officer knew if he might be armed; therefore, it wasn't guaranteed that he was asleep.

"Hands where we can see them!" demanded the officer closest to him.

Cody jolted when the voice blared but his eyes didn't open.

"Up! Up! Up!" the same officer shrieked.

This time he did more than stir. Cody opened his eyes and was immediately dismayed to find four policemen occupying the room and pointing their weapons at him. He wasted very little time sitting up and was about to shove-

"Hands… Now!" yelled the same officer. "Slowly!"

"Man, what's going-"

"Stop right there! Stay where I can see you!" squalled the policeman in the hallway.

Detective Roismann turned to investigate what the uproar was about and saw the door to the room they planned to search next was open halfway. A young adult male stood in the doorway. He must have been jarred awake by them shouting at Cody because he emerged wearing only a pair of boxers and seemed semi consciously disoriented. Roismann believed he was the stepson that Blair mentioned.

The officer in the hallway stepped forward while continuing to point his weapon at Karsyn's face. "Hands in front!"

"Dude, what's your deal?!" Karsyn snapped.

"Moore, stand down!" Roismann ordered.

"I'm not telling you again, kid!" Moore yelled,

ignoring the command.

"Get your fucking gun out of my face!" Karsyn retaliated.

"I gave the order to lower your weapon, officer!" Roismann reminded.

Moore observed Cody for a moment longer before lowering the gun. "I still advise you to keep your hands visible, kiddo."

Karsyn looked toward Detective Roismann standing in the room off to the side and recognized two of the three policemen standing around the bed had their weapons drawn on his father, who was underneath the blanket and looking at them with bewilderment.

"What's going on?" Karsyn questioned.

Detective Roismann sighed. "Right now isn't the time to be looking for answers. Put on some decent clothes so that Moore here can take you downstairs to join your stepmom. We'll talk shortly."

Karsyn glanced at his father. "Dad, what is all of this?!"

Cody remained visibly confused. "I don't-"

"Don't make this hard on yourself, son," Roismann interrupted. "Do what I said or I'll have no choice but to see this fine gentleman place you in cuffs."

Karsyn gnarled his face and heaved a fast dose of inaudible logorrhea off his lips before treading backwards out of the doorway. Officer Moore continued to observe him with his weapon pointed toward the floor and his finger still snared around the trigger.

Detective Roismann turned to the bed again and found that Cody was still buried up to his neck beneath the cover. His perplexed expression hadn't diminished either.

"This can be a very simple situation for you, Mister Undergrove; if you do exactly what we tell you," Detective Roismann encouraged.

"I demand to know what the hell this is about," Cody stated.

"You don't call the shots, pal!" blared the officer standing on the opposite side of the bed.

Cody hunkered down against the headboard when the policeman nearest to him lunged forward and brought the gun closer to his face.

Detective Roismann retreated from aiming his weapon and slipped it inside the holster before retrieving a set of handcuffs that was attached to his tactical belt. "Everything will be explained to you in due time, but for now I need your cooperation. Remove your hands out of the blanket slowly and show us that you're not armed."

"Armed?! Fuck… Really?!" Cody shrieked with disbelief.

"Hands, Mister Undergrove! I highly doubt that you want us to do it for you," Roismann declared.

At first Cody seemed reluctant to do anything but then he likely considered the worst possible outcome because the blanket lifted as he raised his hands beneath it. Once they cleared the blanket, Cody was instantly horrified by the sight. Both hands were covered with dry, flaky blood.

"Oh my god… What the fuck is this?!" he groaned.

Shock may have resonated in his tone but Detective Roismann wasn't buying the damsel in distress charade. He'd dealt with many suspects in his career that put on a good show in an attempt to divert blame. People pretended to be startled. People cried. There were a few instances when people acted like they had fainted prior to arrest. But in the end, roughly ninety-five percent of those same individuals were convicted of the charges filed against them. Statistics and personal knowledge taught him not to trust the visual representation of matters since the genius attribute of a well organized criminal was circumstantial deception.

"I advise you not to make any sudden movements, but what I do need you to do is stand with your back to Officer Bawtrey here," Roismann said, referencing the officer closest to Cody. "Then I want you to calmly put your hands behind you. Don't resist. Don't provoke any sort of altercation. Listen to us and we'll listen to you. Let's work through this together."

"Karsyn!" Cody screamed, ignoring Roismann's request.

"Don't make this difficult," Roismann advised.

"Blair!" Cody yelled, dodging the suggestion and looking all around the room. "Where is she?!"

"Calm down, Mister Undergrove," Detective Roismann encouraged.

"Ella!" Cody persisted in being hysterical.

"Dammit! Enough with your nonsense!" Roismann raged.

"What the fuck is going on?!" Cody roared.

"Bawtrey!" Roismann snapped.

"Someone tell me what the fuck is happening!" Cody squalled.

During his manic outburst, Cody was inattentive of

Officer Bawtrey holstering his weapon to unfasten the handcuffs from his tactical belt. Bawtrey leapt ahead, securing the cuffs with one hand, and wrestled him until he was eventually able to roll him on his stomach. Cody didn't put up much of a fight when getting turned over because he was completely pixelated and still trying to piece together his involvement with the authorities.

Something that Detective Roismann recognized after Bawtrey ripped the blanket away were several long streaks of blood on Cody's bare chest. Cody didn't seem to notice this pivotal detail since he was too caught up in struggling to comprehend what role he played in this procedure. He was obviously being arrested but the fact of the matter simply failed to register with him.

"Get off me! You've got no right treating me this way!" he argued.

Bawtrey mirandized him while yanking his arms behind him and fastening the cuffs.

"You sons of bitches are making a huge mistake! I've not done anything!" Cody disputed.

Officer Bawtrey pulled him off the bed, stood him upright, and then manhandled him in the sense of twisting him around to face Detective Roismann without Cody once making a move on his own. Roismann and the two remaining officers holstered their weapons.

"I'll have your goddamn job!" Cody roared at Roismann. "All of you!"

Detective Roismann placed his hands on his hips and viewed the chaotic backlash to mean nothing more than Cody's failure to confess guilt.

"Mister Undergrove, you are hereby under arrest for

the assault and murder of Ella Pearson," he announced.

This grisly accusation sent Cody into a frenzy. He swung one leg forward - attempting to strike Roismann - but when his foot fell short on making contact, he stood and then kicked ahead with the other one. That foot failed to hit also and he was left in limbo, fighting to regain his balance before Officer Bawtrey slammed him face down on the bed again.

"Stop the bullshit!" Bawtrey advised scornfully.

"What do you mean Ella's dead?!" Cody's inquiry delivered ongoing hostility.

"I am not playing this game with you, Mister Undergrove. You are currently under arrest and in my custody, unless you can provide me with something right now to validate your innocence," Roismann stated.

"Fuck, man! It's obvious that I've not done anything! You saw for yourself, I was asleep!" Cody blasted.

Detective Roismann shook his head. "Taking your word is not how this works."

Cody wriggled beneath Officer Bawtrey's knee pressing the center of his lower back. "Well… Then just how in the hell does this work?!"

"It begins with us taking you down to the station. There, I'll conduct an interview with you and then step aside to allow another detective to do the same. Once we're done with the interviews, then we will stage you in a temporary holding unit while we bring your wife and son in for further questioning. I'm sure you've watched plenty of police shows to know that this is a lengthy process," Roismann concluded.

"You're going to waste my time by keeping me in one of those bullshit drunk tanks?" Cody asked.

Roismann smirked. "I take great pride in being an honest man, Mister Undergrove; therefore, I'd be lying to say that we're going to take you in and then you're going to be right back out. It's highly likely that I'm going to be here, examining the scene and collecting evidence, at least up until sometime midday. So, you can expect it to be a while before I get to you."

"Un-fucking-believable," Cody complained, stabilizing his respirations following the disorderliness.

Officer Bawtrey removed his knee from restricting Cody's movement and dragged him off the bed after taking into consideration that he may have tired himself to the point of unintentional compliance. Cody was then directed to confront Detective Roismann again.

"Shouldn't we get some clothes on him?" Bawtrey asked, on the account that Cody stood in front of them wearing boxers and a pair of white ankle cut socks.

"Yeah," Roismann replied carelessly. He surveyed the clutter strung on the floor from one end of the room to the other and recognized a pair of gray sweatpants next to an almost overfilled basket of dirty laundry in front of the dresser. "Put those on him."

Officer Bawtrey looked in the direction of where he noticed Roismann's eyes targeting and he too spotted the sweatpants. He stepped aside but not too far away from Cody and reached down to grab them.

"Which shirt?" he inquired.

"The fuck if I care," Roismann stated. "If it was just me dealing with him, then I'd drag his ass out naked."

"Well look at you, setting a good example," Cody mentioned sarcastically.

"Being in my custody doesn't come with luxury," Roismann expressed.

Officer Bawtrey rummaged through clothes in the top of the basket and pulled away holding what appeared to be a white A-shirt tangled in itself. He unraveled it and found the cloth severely wrinkled but that didn't matter since jail was not the place to worry about making an impression. He raised it over Cody's head and then pulled it down on him without unfastening the cuffs to let him wear it properly. Cody was surprisingly cooperative with helping Bawtrey fit him into the sweatpants.

"Thanks for that," Bawtrey mentioned, patting him on the shoulder.

"Sure," Cody mumbled. "I mean… What else was I supposed to do?"

"Have shoes?" Detective Roismann interfered.

"They're downstairs. We don't like coming in and tracking debris all over the place. Only the kids do that," Cody responded.

Blair grabbed Karsyn's leg and dabbed her nose with the damp tissue when seeing Detective Roismann turn the corner and begin making his way down the steps. Behind him was Cody. She recognized an expression of bitter confusion on his face; as if he'd been awakened without having any prior knowledge of what was going on. Then she considered that he might actually be broadcasting some form of resting bitch face since he hadn't been conscious long enough for drowsiness to dissipate.

Officer Bawtrey walked behind Cody. Blair was not

surprised that eight policemen had gone upstairs and only two returned. She'd seen countless episodes of primetime crime shows to know what was going on. Unlike Cody, who could never take his eyes off the phone.

"What's going on, Blair?! What the fuck happened to Ella?!" Cody lashed out, midway down the stairs.

Apparently he didn't glimpse into Ella's bedroom while being escorted.

Blair sobbed and it sounded like that was all she could do during the moment.

Karsyn's face suddenly distorted when she squeezed his thigh and broke skin with her fingernails. While she didn't sink them deep enough to draw blood, he did feel a severe sting result. Placing his hand on top of hers and prying between her fingers, he dislodged the nails from staying burrowed inside his leg.

"Goddamnit, Blair!" Cody bawled, descending off the last step and stopping next to Detective Roismann after Officer Bawtrey came down behind him, still holding one of his cuffed wrists. "Tell them! Tell them that I haven't done shit!"

"What did you do to my daughter?!" she lashed out. "Why?! Why?! She didn't deserve this!"

"What are you talking about?!" he asked, with shock rich in his tone. "I was in bed with you! I never got up for anything and you know that! I'd never lay a hand on Ella, or anyone for that matter!"

"You took my baby!" she squalled. "Son of a bitch! You're a fucking monster!"

Karsyn discontinued restraining her hand and embraced it as a means to comfort her the best way he knew how.

"Karsyn, son, tell them! You know I'm not capable of this!" Cody squawked.

Karsyn bowed his head. "Dad, I don't know what happened."

"For fuck sake!" Cody shrilled. "You're both going to sit there and make it out like I did something, really?! I can't believe this!"

Blair ripped her hand from underneath Karsyn's hold and sprang off the couch faster than anyone could register what was going on. She spun around the side and lunged forward, almost reaching Cody with one step.

"I'll kill you! Goddamnit, I will fucking kill you!" she wailed, launching the slimy tissue to the floor before reaching both hands toward his neck.

Luckily, Officer Ryve wasn't far behind and reached her in time to lower her arms before she was capable of grabbing his throat. Detective Roismann could have stopped her but didn't for whatever reason. Officer Ryve pulled her back but she resisted the hint to return to the couch and sit.

"Ella never wanted me to get mixed up with you in the first place, and I should have listened!" she cried. "You're heartless! You ruin lives! She had everything going for her and you took it all away!"

"Come on, ma'am," Officer Ryve urged, continuing to pull her away.

"Would you stop accusing me?!" Cody scolded. "I don't know what happened, but you don't see me pointing the finger at any of you!"

Detective Roismann slipped his hands inside his

pants pockets and glanced over at him. "Honestly, Mister Undergrove, neither of them have raised my suspicion."

Cody looked at him directly. "What the hell is that supposed to mean, exactly?!"

"It means he knows what you did!" Blair blasted.

"Oh, come on!" Cody shrieked, rolling his eyes and then glancing at the ceiling. "Just because I'm an adult male, it gives everyone the right to suspect me?!"

"Actually, I've got every reason to suspect you," Roismann confirmed.

Cody shook his head and provided a tongue in cheek smirk. "You're shitting me, right?"

Detective Roismann glanced at Blair. "Please have a seat, Miss Undergrove. I'm aware this is an extremely difficult time for you right now, but I will speak with you and your stepson in a moment."

After much resistance, she finally surrendered to Officer Ryve's effort to backtrack her to the couch and sit with Karsyn.

Roismann glimpsed at the black mat beside the front door and examined several pairs of footwear. "Are any of these yours?" he inquired.

"Yeah. The crocs are mine," Cody answered.

Detective Roismann stepped aside to clear the way. "All right. Go ahead and get them on so that we can get down to business."

Cody went forward as directed. "Man, I'm telling you this is a big mistake."

"Just do what you're told. If we find that you're in the clear, then you've got nothing to worry about," Officer Bawtrey commented, while continuing to follow protocol by holding one of his remanded wrists.

Detective Roismann waited for him to be escorted from the premises before approaching the couch. He examined Blair and sort of sympathized with her anguish because it was pouring out of her so much that she lacked the ability to hold herself together even for a moment. Then he checked Karsyn and distinguished a peculiar unease about him. Karsyn recognized his own undesired nervousness and slipped both hands between his legs to avoid anyone noticing them tremble.

It bothered him that he might be the one person that knew what really happened to Ella. Jake propositioned him about wanting a sensual encounter with her earlier. He referenced Blair also. Karsyn denied accepting either opportunity as a form of payback for the fifteen-hundred dollars he owed in return for getting fronted narcotics on about a handful of instances.

Maybe Jake had found a way to break inside the house and the only thing that interested him was finding Ella's room. Perhaps she put up a fight when he attempted having his way with her and the only way to keep her quiet was by going to fatal extremes. Karsyn didn't doubt that his estranged supplier was capable of murder. Jake did go as far as to pull a gun on him and threaten to use it. The inability to assault Blair because his father was in bed made perfect sense. What he could not justify was the reason why his father's hands were covered with blood.

Karsyn felt that he couldn't reach out in his father's defense because if he mentioned Jake, then it would risk putting the spotlight on his own illegal activities. The fact that he might be the middleman in this mess caused him to feel significantly nervous.

"What's your name, son?" Detective Roismann asked.

Karsyn made eye contact with him but for only a brief moment. "Karsyn, sir."

"Karsyn. All right. Tell me something, kiddo. Do you play sports and get good grades?" Roismann questioned.

Karsyn tightened his legs against his hands. "No and no. I'm not in school anymore. Graduated."

"A high school graduate. Must mean you've got a decent head on your shoulders. Are you working anywhere?" Roismann asked, after noticing a slight quiver in the young man's voice.

Karsyn shook his head. "Unfortunately, no, sir."

"Ah, I see. Sponging off your dad and stepmom here until they force you to find employment?" Roismann supposed.

"No. It's nothing like that," Karsyn said nervously.

Detective Roismann leaned down on one knee in front of him. "I assume that you have no idea what went on here tonight?"

Karsyn glanced at him for another quick moment. "Sorry. I was in my room and didn't know that anything was happening. If I did, then I would have come out and done something."

Roismann squinted while still observing him. "I need you to help me understand something, Karsyn. Not long ago you were loud and mouthy with us, but now you're almost afraid to speak. Why is that?"

Karsyn sensed his false calm presentation was

becoming more difficult to sustain. He couldn't look at Detective Roismann because he knew anxiety would have his head shuddering if he did. The fear of getting busted for his narcotics addiction was on the cusp of leading him into an emotional meltdown.

"I didn't know what was going on. You guys showed up with your guns pulled. One was aimed at me. How else was I supposed to react?" he stated.

Detective Roismann bowed his head. "That's legit."

When he looked up again, Roismann directed his attention to Blair. "Blair, or do you prefer that I call you Miss Undergrove?"

"Blair," she answered quietly.

"Okay. Blair, do you know if your daughter had any disagreements with your husband recently?" he inquired, standing slowly.

"Every day was a struggle with those two. They never saw eye to eye," she replied.

"Is it possible that one of these disputes could have been serious enough to provoke him to want to harm her?" he asked.

She swayed her head and sniffled. "No. They were always going at each other over little things. Nothing major."

"They basically just failed to coexist?" he asked.

"Correct," she stated.

"Was there anything specific about your daughter that may have led him to lash out in a fit of rage?" he questioned.

"Rage, no. Desire, maybe," she confessed.

"Huh?" Karsyn sounded off upon hearing the news.

Detective Roismann's face took on a perplexed state. "What do you mean?"

She laid her hand on Karsyn's leg and patted it twice before looking at him and frowning. "I'm sorry, sweetheart. This isn't something I wanted you to know."

After her admission about keeping it a secret, she looked at Detective Roismann and sighed heavily. "Ugh… Okay. Jesus, I don't know where to begin. Ella was involved with something that I honestly didn't approve of her doing. I didn't find out about it for quite some time and I'll explain how I did in a moment. Anyway, she was doing some gig as an online cam girl; making lucrative videos and revealing photos of a provocative nature. I never got the chance to speak with her about it, but I believe it's one of those sites that men have to pay in order to be able to subscribe. I learned about this several months ago when I found out-"

"Yo, Roismann! Where do you need us?!" blared a man's voice from across the room.

Detective Roismann turned and saw an additional handful of policemen, a crime scene photographer, and the medical examiner standing all together barely inside the house. A few of them hadn't been with the department long enough to investigate a homicide since murder wasn't something that ordinarily rattled the community; however, all of them appeared as though they had never been called to the scene of a crime. Even the medical examiner seemed clueless, and Roismann knew for a fact that he'd dealt with every possible scenario in the past two and a half decades.

Detective Roismann pointed at the top of the stairs. "Lone door on the right!"

Then he turned and glimpsed at Officer Moore standing behind the backrest where Karsyn was seated. "Do you mind giving them a walk through and explaining what we found on arrival?"

Officer Moore stepped out of position and careened in the direction of late arrivals. "Come on, guys! I'm going to walk you through what we found."

Detective Roismann turned to Blair again. "So, your daughter was an amatuer model and you believe it has something to do with what happened tonight?"

Blair sniffled and choked back what might have turned into another bout of uncontrollable sorrow. "I know it has everything to do with this."

Roismann crossed his arms. "Explain."

"A few months ago I found out that Cody had been looking at pictures and watching videos of her on whatever repulsive site she joined. He didn't just go there sometimes. I browsed his account information and learned that he was subscribed to her page; meaning that he got notified whenever she had something new to share," she disclosed.

Detective Roismann stayed silent. Maybe he strongly conceived the notion that she wasn't done providing imperative information without his request.

Blair did continue. "My daughter. The same beautiful young lady that he vowed to protect with me. His own stepdaughter. I can't comprehend how or why he did these things. He'd watch her do normal everyday things and then turn right around and go online to see her portray herself in ways that no woman should ever consider. He's sick. That's all it really boils down to. Just fucking sick."

Finally, Detective Roismann inquired, "How did

you come to know that your husband was a member of whatever thing she was doing?"

"I found it on his phone after noticing that he was spending too much time on it. He was in the shower one evening and left his phone on the bedside table. Being curious about what he spent all his time doing, I picked it up to have a look. Didn't take but only a second to see what I hoped I wouldn't. The internet browser popped up and revealed the last thing he looked at was Ella's content. I will never get the image I saw that day out of my head," she answered.

"And how long ago did you notice that he was doing this?" Roismann questioned, conducting a mild cross examination based on the grounds of her telling him that it was three months.

"Three months. Could have been two and a half but no less," she clarified.

"Oh my god," Karsyn spoke under his breath.

Detective Roismann shot a stern glance at him. "You had no idea this was going on, right?"

"Yes," Karsyn gasped.

Roismann's brows perked. "Yes?"

"No. I mean, yes - I didn't know," Karsyn expressed anxiously.

"Why did you not confront him when you found out?" Roismann asked Blair.

She let out a nonverbal form of brokenhearted despair before replying, "I don't know. I guess I was waiting for a more appropriate time because so much was going on that I didn't want to create conflict. I should have said something. I should have taken Ella and got the hell away from here, actually."

Detective Roismann turned and paced for just a short distance before returning to the couch. "Do you know where his phone is right now?"

"On the table beside the bed. That's where it stays during the night," she communicated straight away.

"Good," he remarked. "I'll be sure to grab it and have it searched for any supporting data that might be helpful during the course of our investigation. Although visiting a site in order to see lewd images of your daughter is purely contemptible, it is not a crime given the fact she isn't a minor. But he may have very easily researched a particular idea or expressed his thoughts with someone over a text message. Either scenario is a reason for me to take out a warrant and scour for a motive."

"What happens if you search through his phone but do not find anything incriminating?" she asked.

Roismann sighed. "I believe there is enough circumstantial evidence based on our initial discovery that he isn't going to walk away from this one. Plus we're going to take a DNA sample from your daughter since it's ninety-nine percent likely she was assaulted. We'll get a sample from your husband today as well. If he doesn't agree to participate willingly, then I will issue a warrant for collection."

"DNA?" Karsyn's voice rattled apprehensively.

Detective Roismann uncrossed his arms and slid his hands inside the pants pockets again. "Is that a problem?"

"No," Karsyn answered quickly, shaking his head at the same time. "It's just… I mean, that's a lot of digging when you've got all the answers already, right?"

Roismann smirked. "There is more to an investigation than speculation. You've got to have facts."

Karsyn didn't say any more. He looked around everywhere except at Detective Roismann because he knew his eyes would tattletale the epitome of his agitation.

Detective Roismann pulled one hand from his pocket and scratched the corner of his mouth. "I noticed something earlier and didn't mention it, but I'm curious - what happened to your lip?"

"Oh," Karsyn sounded out instantly. "That's nothing."

"Did you and your father get into a little scuffle recently?" Roismann asked.

"No. We've never had a physical altercation. I don't think we've ever had a serious disagreement," Karsyn replied, squishing his sweaty hands together and grinding his fingers between each other. "Me and a friend were horseplaying. I ended up stepping too close at one point and he landed a jab."

"He must've given some hard swings to bust you open like that," Roismann articulated.

Karsyn smiled uncomfortably. "Yeah. That's what I get for roughhousing with someone that helped lead our football team to the state championship back in the day."

Detective Roismann studied him while both experience and gut feeling insinuated to him that something wasn't adding up. Karsyn may have done a good job concealing his hands but the lasting vibration in his voice affirmed that not everything was spoken with honesty. Roismann didn't know what he might want to hide and he didn't suspect the boy had involvement in Ella's murder, but there were details about happenings that Karsyn obviously didn't want known.

"Is there anything else you need from us?" Blair asked.

"Yes. At some point I'll have Officer Ryve transport you and your stepson down to the station for me to conduct a more thorough interview. I'll ask many of the same questions I've asked here but the next round will be recorded as official statements," Roismann retorted.

"Oh, okay. I've never dealt with law enforcement in my life; so, I don't know what procedures are or how things play out from this moment," she mentioned.

Detective Roismann glanced at Officer Ryve but only long enough for Ryve to look at him directly. Then he gazed down at Blair again. "I am going to go out of my way and break the procedure in how we typically handle matters. We're going to be in and out of here during all hours of the morning. There will be people leaving and new ones arriving, such as individuals that specialize in cleaning the scene once our job is finished. So, there's going to be a lot of commotion. Seeing that you're pregnant, I don't think it's reasonable for you to witness things that would cause you to endure more trauma than you've suffered already."

"Umm… Okay," she said, uncertain about what he was implying.

"I could go ahead and have my officer take you to the station but it would be a long, uncomfortable while before me or anyone else was able to accommodate either of you. Plus I really don't have a place for you to hang out for that length of time, unless you wouldn't mind waiting in a temporary holding cell," he added.

"No thanks," Karsyn grumbled.

"It isn't something I'd recommend anyway," Roismann stated.

"Then what do you suggest we do?" Blair questioned.

"I don't know of anywhere we can go."

Roismann jingled whatever was in his pocket. "Are you familiar with Budget Palace? It's the motel about a mile up the road from the courthouse."

"More like the Red Roach Resort," Karsyn muttered.

A brief moment of silence passed before Blair replied. "Yeah. I know the place. I've never stayed there though."

"I know the family that runs it. They're a good bunch and are understanding. In fact, they've helped me in a lot of situations. What I'm going to do is have Officer Ryve take the two of you there until I'm ready to go more in depth with your interviews. You'll be waiting somewhere warm and out of the way of what we'll have going on here," Roismann aired.

"I don't have the money for that," she gasped.

"It's okay. I'm sending you. No one has to worry about paying for anything. Officer Ryve will explain that you need somewhere to rest for a few hours and then you'll be taken good care of," he confirmed.

"Are you sure?" she asked.

He nodded. "I've known them for a long time. If I send you, then that is where you'll stay."

"Umm… Can we change clothes?" Karsyn asked.

"Unfortunately, that is not an option," Roismann declared, observing him in a T-shirt and pair of mesh shorts. "This whole place is pretty much a crime scene. You'll be okay wearing what you've got on."

Blair reached over and rubbed the area above his knee; it was basically the same spot she clawed with her fingernails earlier. Then she looked at him with an emotionally painstricken frown. "We'll be alright."

"Do you mind sharing a room?" Roismann asked, eyeing her.

"No," she replied, almost without hesitation. "Realistically, each other is all we've got."

Detective Roismann peered at Officer Ryve. "Alrighty. The last thing I need is for the two of you to slide into your shoes so that this officer here can take you to the motel."

"Can I not drive us there?" she inquired, seemingly surprised by the idea of having to ride with a policeman.

"Nope. I am not allowed to let you do that," he commented. "Officer Ryve will take you like I mentioned. He'll wait outside. When I radio him that I'm ready, then he will bring you to the station and I'll proceed to interview the two of you extensively, one at a time. Once I've finished taking your statements, then it should be appropriate for you to return home. He will bring you back as well."

"Okay," she said, and was the first to make a move off the couch. "The motel it is, I guess."

CHAPTER NINE

"Y'all sit tight. This will only take a sec," Officer Ryve publicized, opening the door and stepping out of the vehicle.

Karsyn waited for the door to close before reacting after a long period of having to keep his mouth shut. "What the actual fuck is going on? I got a glimpse of Ella and all I really saw was blood everywhere. How did we not hear anything? A scream. Shout. Something."

"Cody murdered my baby girl. That's what happened," Blair stated, staring through the windshield and into the bay window of the front office. There were no curtains or blinds covering the glass. Just a large bare window offering a view of the room. She saw that it didn't take long for Officer Ryve to step inside and approach the counter. He glanced around a few times before she recognized his mouth open and assumed he was calling out to someone for assistance.

She finished answering him by saying, "Ella probably didn't scream because she didn't know what was happening. She probably wasn't even awake during it all. She came home completely wasted last night. Your father wanted me to say something to her but I didn't because she was in no shape to carry a conversation. She wouldn't have remembered anything if I did try talking to her."

"What makes you think my dad did it?" he asked.

"Because he got out of bed early this morning and that was unusual. At first I thought he might have gone to the bathroom but he was away for too long. Aware of the sick shit he was doing on his phone, I waited until he came back to bed and fell asleep before I went to check on her. Something just didn't feel right and I needed to know she was okay. I guess her being drunk and the fact that he was looking at her inappropriately made me sensitive to the idea something wasn't right. And it wasn't. I found Ella with her shorts pulled down and shirt raised. Beneath all that blood was my naked child."

"Dad might be an asshole at times but he wouldn't hurt anybody," Karsyn heaved.

"You wouldn't imagine he'd get creepy over his step daughter either," she retaliated.

Continuing to peer through the window, she watched an elderly woman enter the office from a doorway leading into a side room behind the counter. The lady braced herself with one hand on the countertop as she approached. A big smile warmly welcomed Officer Ryve and then her mouth began to move as if she was jumping straight to business. After Ryve and the woman exchanged a few lighthearted facial expressions, she glanced out the window and studied the police cruiser. Blair suspected the observation was a result of him explaining her and Karsyn's predicament without going into full detail.

"All of this is unbelievable. I'm having a hard time processing what I saw when I passed her bedroom. It all happened so quickly," Karsyn mentioned.

"Be glad you didn't get a close up view of what

happened to her. It's inconceivable. I didn't know a person could harbor the evil I saw unleashed on her," she confessed.

"I'm just in shock," he said.

"You honestly didn't know what Ella was doing online?" she asked, witnessing the woman hand over what she believed was a room key to Officer Ryve.

"I knew she was doing something but I didn't know what. She never gave me any details. The only thing she said was that she was making some decent cash outside of her regular job," Karsyn replied.

"I should have confronted them both. Everything could and should have gone differently. Now I don't know what to do," she said.

"If dad did this, then he doesn't stand a chance. They're going to put him away for life."

"I pray the bastard rots in hell," she snapped in retaliation to his statement.

He leaned forward and looked with her through the steel wire mesh installed to protect the officer from possible dangers pertaining to arrestees. "I know it's not the right time but we've got to tell him. He's going to spend the rest of his life thinking-"

"Sshhh," she interrupted, watching Officer Ryve exit the office. "We'll talk when we get in the room."

Karsyn noticed him coming forward and didn't speak another word.

Officer Ryve stopped next to the rear passenger door which happened to be the side Ella was on. He opened it and stepped out of the way to clear the exit.

"Okay. Looks like she's putting you up in Room

Twelve," he pronounced.

She scooted out of the backseat and stood beside him. "I know that detective said all of this is going to take a while, but how long would you say if you had to guess?"

He sighed. "I can't say for sure because I honestly don't know. I've never dealt with this type of situation."

"Oh. Okay. I really need to make some calls to family but I left my phone at home. Guess I'll worry about that later," she said.

He disregarded her statement by leaning down and looking inside the back of the vehicle. "Do you want to slide out over here or want me to come around to your side?"

"Nah, man," Karsyn blurted, and scooted toward the passenger side exit. "I can get out over there."

Officer Ryve closed the door following Karsyn's departure from the cruiser and raised the mag stripe style of room key in front of them. "This is your room key. I'll be waiting right here. I'm not going anywhere. When Detective Roismann gives me the go ahead, then I'll come knock on the door to let you guys know it's time to hit the station."

Karsyn took the key from him. "You did say Room Twelve, right?"

"Room Twelve," Ryve answered.

Blair stood in place, seemingly unsure of what to do, until Karsyn raised the key card in front of her face. "Are you ready?" he asked.

"Oh. Uh… Yeah," she replied, snapping out of whatever slight daze.

Karsyn swiped the key and the mechanics that

controlled the locking mechanism clicked. He pressed the handle down halfway and pushed the door open to a dark room. Then he stepped aside while continuing to hold it open and glanced back at her, silently signaling for her to go ahead of him.

She reached inside and flipped the light on before crossing the doorway. The room wasn't extravagant and she expected this already since Budget Palace was nowhere near resembling a Hilton or Hyatt franchise. The dead grass color carpet reminded her of something straight out of the 1970's. Nothing about the color scheme was eye-catching. The Queen bed on the left side of the room was covered by an egg yoke yellow comforter. The bedside table was barely large enough to support the lamp and corded phone. Across from the bed was a wide dresser with an older generation flatscreen television on top. On the far side of the room was a narrow door that she assumed led into the bathroom.

She looked across her left side and recognized a round wooden table with two chairs. Positioned at the center was a cafeteria style lunch tray providing a coffee pot with its electrical cord wrapped around the handle, two small plastic cups in individual packaging, several pouches of sugar, containers of creamer, and two bags of coffee.

To the left side of the table was the window overlooking the parking lot. She stepped in front of the window and scanned the view outside. The place was practically deserted but she wasn't surprised since the motel had the reputation for being indecent. Officer Ryve's cruiser was parked on the far right end of the lot from her angle. She didn't see him anywhere and assumed he had jumped back inside the squad car. Where he was sitting he could not see any activity that would soon transpire inside the room, but she felt it was in her best interest not to take that risk and reached across both sides of the window to snatch each piece of the burnt orange curtain and pull them together to ensure their privacy.

Karsyn shut the door and turned to discover something he didn't expect. Blair held one hand up and was pointing a finger as though she was about to scold him. Her facial expression spoke volumes but no part of it hinted at oppression. Every skin distorting wrinkle along with the gleam in her eyes insinuated that she might potentially be enraged.

"We're not telling him anything. Are you crazy? All that would accomplish is get all the attention directed at us and I'm not inclined to stand back and watch you cause that to happen," she spat.

She was livid, sure enough. This sudden shift in mood took him by surprise because she was utterly overwhelmed by anguish and despondency just a while ago.

"We owe it to ourselves to tell him the truth for once. If something happens and he walks away a free man after everything that's happened, then what are you going to do? Are you going to live happily ever after with him - knowing what you share is a lie? What about me? Me, Blair? What do you expect me to do… Turn my back on the truth?" he asked inhospitably.

She lowered her hand and stepped away from the window. "We don't have to say anything because he isn't going to be in our way. I saw what he did to Ella. The police have seen it too. We've got nothing to worry about."

Karsyn shook his head with disbelief. "Seriously, I can't believe we're talking about this right now. Your daughter was slaughtered in the middle of the night, and your husband - my father - has been arrested on suspicion. Those are the things that should concern us right now; not this talk about how the situation is beneficial."

"I'm not trying to sound insensitive by making the incident favorable. You said that you want to come clean about everything, and I'm saying there's no need. That's the only point I'm trying to make," she specified.

He turned his back to her and walked across the room halfway before stopping in front of the bed. Then he lowered his head and brought one hand against his forehead while staring aimlessly at the floor.

"I don't know what the fuck to do. This is some deep shit. I've got to get the hell away from here. I do know that much. Once we get out of the police station, I'm gone. I'm packing my shit and getting away from here, somehow. I don't have anywhere to go but I'll figure it out. I'm not running to my mom. I don't want anything to do with her and her new beau. Fuck that," he expressed.

"You can't leave," she blurted out quickly. "I need you here."

"Blair, I can't stay. If I did, then it's just a matter of time before they come for me. You don't know the shit I've gotten myself in."

"You can't just walk away from us. We need you."

He turned and confronted her. She appeared slightly blurry due to tears swelling in his eyes. "I'm sorry. I really don't want to but I've got no choice."

She reached both hands against the bottom of her stomach. "We need to raise this child together. I don't want to be in the situation years down the road where I have to explain that getting scared and going on the run meant more to you than sticking by my side and raising a family. Our family. Please, Karsyn, stay and be the man that I know you are."

He took the same hand that caressed his forehead a moment ago and frantically brushed along the top of his head. "Come with me. We'll get as far away from Pearisburg as possible. Start a new life someplace where nobody knows us. I'll find a job and we can buy a nice house. Whatever it takes, let's get away from here."

She frowned. "Our lives are here. My family is here. We have a home to call our own. I've got a great job that I'm going to have to return to at some point. Everything we need is right here; so, there is no reason to abandon what we have and start over."

"Dammit, Blair. I said that I've got to get out of this place. You're going to lose me if we don't."

"Karsyn, we are going to be okay," she spoke confidently, prior to approaching him. "I'm not going to let anything happen to you."

"Trust me, it's too late," he informed her.

She withdrew both hands from her stomach and touched the side of his face with one and seized his hand with the other. "I'll protect you at all costs. I might not look like I'm capable of much but I can scrap with the best of them."

He leaned his head into her affectionate touch. "This isn't something you or I can take on. Everything is stacked against me."

She brushed her thumb back and forth against his cheek. "Believe me when I say that I'll do whatever it takes to make damn certain that you play an important role in our child's life. Whoever you think might come after you will have to go through me, and they'll not get far. You've got nothing to worry about."

Karsyn sighed. There was more doubt in his mind than her words could comfort. "I'm not worried about who might come after me. It's the seriousness of the matter that-"

"What are you afraid of?" she interrupted.

"It's not something I want to talk about with you. Even if I tried, then it would become a conversation too complicated for either of us," he mentioned.

"You're involved with that one dude again, aren't you?" she asked.

"What are you talking about?" he replied with a rhetorical question.

"You might be capable of hiding the obvious from your father but I see things clearly. I'm aware it's the same car always showing up in front of the house. I know they're giving you some type of drug because your pupils dilate. I know every time that you're coming down because you get moody as fuck and are a nervous wreck. I noticed your lip was busted when you came back inside the house last night but I didn't call you out on it because I didn't want your father exploding on you about it. You can try convincing yourself all you want that I don't know you're using substance, but I do. Now tell me, where are you getting the money to support this habit? I know they aren't just giving it to you because you're such a good friend," she responded.

He squinted and then looked away by bowing his head with disappointment. "Shit… You really do pay attention to details."

"You haven't answered the question. How are you paying for it?"

"That's the problem. I'm not. He's been fronting me for quite a while and is now on my ass about it. I will pay it back. I don't know how but I'll figure it out."

"How much do you owe?"

He shook his head. "Fifteen hundred, if I did the math correctly."

Sudden shock spawned solely from hearing the amount caused her to squeeze his hand. "Fifteen hundred dollars. What the hell are you thinking?"

"It's insane, I know. I felt that I was always needing something and he kept supplying. I never meant for things to get out of hand," he confessed.

She eased her hand beneath his chin and raised his head to have him look at her again. "We'll take care of it. I'll pay the fifteen hundred to get him off your back. You've got to promise me something though," she said.

"You don't have to clean up my mess," he stated.

"Promise me something," she stressed.

"Okay. What's that?" he inquired.

"I take care of your debt and then you step away from dealing with him. No more getting yourself strung out. You are going to live responsibly and prioritize the important things in life," she addressed.

"It isn't that easy. You can't expect me to just walk

away from the only thing I've known all my life without there being struggles," he confessed.

"I do." She pulled his hand to her stomach and guided him to rub the side of its bulge. "You've got more than yourself to worry about."

He turned quiet. Several thoughts beyond his illegal involvements crossed his mind. His father's arrest troubled him because he still believed that Cody played no part in the gruesome atrocity. Ella's unfortunate fate was severely bothersome. The private affair with Blair that resulted in her getting pregnant burdened him for the reason that they'd have to continue in secret or else they would catch the spotlight as primary suspects. The fact that no one was aware of their relationship bothered him as well. He hated having to pretend in front of others that he despised the woman he actually loved.

"What are we going to do if dad gets out?" he asked.

"Stop worrying about that too. They have no reason to let him out. He raped and murdered my child. All proof is there that he was obsessed," she stated.

Karsyn shut his eyes.

Rape-

Murder-

The words alone brought him to shudder.

"Nothing will come between us," she said.

"Okay. But let's say the court fucks up and has to release him for whatever reason, then what do we do? We won't be able to continue this because I'm not going to stick around and watch him raise my kid. Do you have a plan if we're put in that situation?" he asked.

"We wouldn't need one," she answered. "I'd tell him that I want a separation given everything that has happened, and I would get my own place for you to come over anytime you want. You can tell him that you got a night shift job so that you can spend more time with me. Once the divorce is finalized, then I would want you to move in with me. We will raise this child together, no matter what."

Regardless of his discomfort and perplexity, Karsyn grinned. "This right here is the reason I love you."

"Why is that?" she catechized.

He pulled her closer to him. "You're fucking crazy."

Blair giggled and didn't become quiet until their lips met for a long fiery kiss. Emotions heated so quickly that she was gasping for air during instances when his tongue pulled back from wriggling inside her mouth. She was no longer able to control her body since it began squirming with anticipation. She slid both hands onto his shoulders and submitted herself to the strength of a much younger man. She felt the hunger in him to feast on the passion of his stepmom reveal itself during the occasional moments that he bit her lip.

Karsyn moved his hand from her stomach and reached around her back before pulling her toward him. His other hand touched the side of her face to glide behind her neck and sneak up slowly into her hair. He wreathed it all around his hand and pulled her head back, biting her lip at the same time and not releasing until the distance separated his teeth from flesh.

"Are you going to tell your family about us?" he

asked.

"I will eventually," she groaned.

"When?" he fired back.

"I don't know," she spoke quietly, squeezing his shoulders in a way of signaling how badly she wanted him to take her without further interregnum.

"If they don't accept?" he continued questioning.

Blair sighed and growled afterward. "They'll see it as an abomination but I don't care. I want you. I need you. I have you. That's all that matters."

"I want you no matter what anyone says," he spilled in one breath.

She shivered excitedly and coasted her hands behind his neck. Karsyn leaned down and buried his face upon the mild fragrance of stale sweat dried on her skin. He licked alongside the collarbone and maneuvered up slowly beneath her ear. Then he grasped the bottom of her earlobe with a gentle bite and hold. She moaned softly as he pulled.

Still yanking a handful of tangled hair, he twisted her around so that her back faced the bed. He groped the hindside of her hip and let go of her ear.

"It probably isn't the right time for this," he whispered, dragging his nose down the side of her neck.

"No. This is exactly what I need right now," she gasped. "It will help take my mind off things."

Her approval to let things continue prompted him to steer her backwards onto the bed and lay next to her since he didn't want to be on top and place too much pressure on her stomach. The hand concealed inside the large knot of hair had since pulled away and was now brushing the side of her face, while the other must have remained against her back since it hadn't been brought forward to explore. His face hovered above her own only seconds before he swooped down and locked lips with her again. She ran both hands up and down his back after jiggling free the one that was wedged between him and the bed.

"Uhh… Yeah," she sounded out during the brief moment when their mouths parted.

Karsyn pulled his hand from her face and reached down, grabbing what felt like the entire breast underneath the tank top. He noticed she wasn't wearing a bra by how the swelled nipple poked beneath the fabric. He treated the whole breast aggressively for a moment - pressing, pinching, pulling - before releasing and drifting down her side. His hand sank below her waist and crossed the top of her leg to reach the inner thigh. Every inch of the way was a smooth transit across the fabric of her pajama pants and he didn't stop until his hand burrowed in her crotch.

Blair gasped.

She moved one leg aside and broadened the space between them.

Karsyn slid his hand up slowly and then moved down gradually again, bending his fingers inward and applying pressure while grinding between her thighs. The fast growing anticipation to explore that region concealed inside her pants instigated a sudden throb in his shorts. This awakening of excitement cascading throughout his penis provoked him to reach above the waistband of her pants. Swathing his tongue around hers, Karsyn felt his adrenalin lead to kissing more aggressively while his fingers struggled to claw underneath the elastic band. He recalled that these pants were much easier to pry his way inside about two months ago, but this pregnancy had caused her stomach to expand quite a bit ever since. After digging at her skin for a short while, he finally succeeded in pressing his fingers underneath the waistband and reached further to scrape against warm silk blanketing her crotch.

Blair broke away from kissing. "Mmm… Baby, you know how to always feel so good."

He lowered his mouth below her chin and she arched her head to feel his tongue prod down the front of her throat. Relying on the warmth inside her pajama bottoms to fuel his hunger, he brushed his fingers to one side of their narrow material and massaged damp skin next to her thigh.

She moaned and breathed heavily as he groped the furthest outer region of her vagina.

"I want you," she gasped.

His breathing intensified. He noticed this by how hard and repetitive it struck her neck before bouncing back in his face.

"This isn't right." He cast doubt while reflecting on everything involving Ella's grisly murder and his father's shocking arrest.

"Don't stop," she mumbled, and rubbed his back more assertively. "I've gone for too long without feeling you. It's been killing me to see you and not have this."

Continuing to explore between her thighs, he dragged the narrow silk aside and noticed that the area underneath wasn't smooth. Not allowing this temporary discomfort to distract his intent, he glided his fingers across the bristly terrain and stopped after poking the puffy folds at the top of her pussy. He penetrated the lips when pressing down and his fingers became coated by the slippery sap oozing out of her crotch. Brushing his two fingers up and covering the mushy clit with the same sticky lubricant that slickened the flesh inside the folds of her vagina, he applied pressure before insensitively jerking those fingers from left to right and back again.

"Oh… Oh… Oh… Fuck!" Blair shrieked as the frenzy of arousal climaxed and took her over completely.

He moved to the bottom of her pussy and paused when reaching the top of the slender opening. He spread the slimy lips before covering the opening without slipping inside.

Blair wriggled next to him. She raised her hips and squirmed her pussy against his fingers until she was no longer able to hold herself elevated and crashed her ass on the bed.

"Don't stop!" she groaned, having a hard time expressing herself because all that she seemed capable of doing easily was groaning and gasping. "Uh- Yeah. Right there."

Karsyn forced two fingers inside the tight fit, and because they were oiled by vaginal mucus, it was less complicated for him to push knuckles deep inside. He pulled back slowly - pausing once the rear edge of his fingernails approached the outside of the cavity - and then he thrust forward again. A quiet sloshing sound announced just how aroused she had become by his gentleness.

Blair reached down and grabbed his shorts. She groped his dick, discovering how ultimately stimulated it was by his own excitement. She squirmed more frequently as emotional euphoria escalated to the point that she could not lay there and deny herself of the craving for any longer.

"I want you," she gasped, squeezing his dick. "Inside me."

He abstained from nibbling on her neck long enough to say, "I will."

As if gripping his penis from outside the shorts wasn't enough, she slid to the top and then sailed inside them. She brushed along a drizzle of precum and smeared it against her wrist while making her way down the shaft. Getting a firm grip on its bottom, she tugged up slowly beneath the head and went back down above the balls just as gradually. She moaned desirously as the veins inside his penis pulsated against her hand. After a couple of more strokes his cock twitched. Blair licked her lips and raised those thighs. Impatience caused her to start jerking him off faster and with more bellicosity.

"Fuck, babe," she groaned. "Don't make me wait."

Karsyn didn't speak. His pace of scraping her soft interior increased to match the speed of her yanking his dick. Despite how awkward her hold on him was inside the shorts, it felt so good that he knew he'd cum on her fingers if she kept going. He bit her neck harder than any time prior and held the pressure with intent to mark a visual memory of their rapture.

Suddenly his mind guided him into reminiscing about a dark place.

Not only dark in atmosphere but in events as well.

His thoughts took him creeping inside the minimally moonlit room where he stood in front of the bed. Ella laid in front of him. She was asleep with her shirt raised above her breasts. He squeezed them - pinched their nipples. His penis swelled and throbbed in his pants before the hunger to take advantage of the circumstance and have her for himself encouraged one hand to shirk down between her legs. Ella's pussy was disparagingly dry; following an innumerous amount of fervid chafes it became soppy.

"No," he blurted. This unexpected recollection brought agitation that displaced him mentally. "I can't. We can't…"

"Yes, we can," she hissed, clawing up the back of his shirt and speeding the handjob. "And we are."

Plah. Plah. Plah. Plah.

Karsyn squinted his shut eyes even tighter and unintentionally allowed his tormented mind to steer him far from the sound of her gooey cum glazed hand battering his nutsack.

His thoughts returned him to Ella's room. There he had advanced from exploring with his hands to holding the strap of a belt buckled around her throat. He thrust himself deep between her thighs and the rhythm intensified as he reflected how long he'd fantasized about this particular occasion. Of course, everything he imagined never involved her unconscious but he had to take advantage of the situation when it was presented. Ella never would have let him fuck her willingly; she was nothing more than a cocktease that fed his interest by prancing around the house, dressed in ways that she knew would grab his attention. He knew she was aware of what she was doing, and he was weak enough to surrender to the erotic voodoo which resulted in him masturbating on a regular basis. But he finally got his wish and it felt so much fucking better than he ever dreamed.

With the visualization of that belt fastened around Ella's throat still playing out in his mind, Karsyn dipped his fingers until his entire palm covered Blair's pussy. Excitement that he received from securing the leather so tight around Ella's neck reinvented itself in the way he oppressively scrunched the handful of lubricious flesh. He wanted to end this progressive sexcapade due to the mental recurrence but his body was obviously noncompliant.

"God, yesss!" Blair groaned, trembling all over as a result of his fierce clasp.

Karsyn didn't flench. He did not ease up on the pressure and his fingers remained deeply entombed.

"DNA. Sample."

"DNA. Collection."

Detective Roismann's haunting voice echoed those fearful words throughout his head.

He desperately wanted to break away from his involvement with Blair but in the end he was too caught up in the tingling excitement of what might eventually pass in the form of him busting a nut. What happened due to this incitement was that he let go of mashing her pussy and picked up ramming it with the same lack of sympathy he showed toward Ella.

Blair slung her head back further and raised her shoulders when the assault between her legs became everything she spent months secretly daydreaming about. Turning her face away from him and grinding her teeth to prevent the risk of making any sound that might extend outside the room, she brought her hand to the top of his shaft and held steady while constricting him with every ounce of energy she had in her to exert. She believed she had so much of a tight grip that the head of his dick was likely purple at this point, but she was in such an odd position that she couldn't whip it out and take a look.

The feeling of his fingers reacting like pistons, plummeting constantly at the lowest depth within their reach, filled her with sensations she forgot existed. Anytime that Cody was in the mood, she didn't really experience anything and rarely got off since the only thing that interested him was achieving his own ejaculation. Of course, it never did take him long to shoot his load either. Most of the time he lasted for only five minutes; however, during those rare instances that he was forced to pause and wait out a leg cramp, then his endurance allowed him to perform for about eight minutes. One ailment that he was never able to overcome was having sex with just a partially firm erection, and the fact that she got used to getting uncomfortably plugged by a half flimsy penis played a large role in all of the reasons she could not orgasm. She assumed that his pathetic efforts to try satisfying her was the cause for their lovelife plunging next to nothing.

Fortunately, she didn't suffer these disappointing drawbacks with Karsyn. He wasn't just always stone hard and ready to explode but he also executed the stamina to conquer her senses for longer than an hour. Things he made her feel were incredible. Aside from being persuaded that she was wanted and appreciated, Blair encountered enthusiasm that overloaded her with mental youthfulness. She dueled with herself all the time about not gushing too soon and in every event she almost squirted at the beginning because his palpitating shaft hyper excited her

upon insertion.

She heaved a muffled groan while gritting her teeth.

All control of her body was absent, considering how she persisted convulsing periodically.

Preserving the firm grip of his cock, she shoved down and slammed his balls with an intensity that caused him to screech and spew curse words immediately. Then she tugged and he howled once more.

Immense ecstasy surging throughout her mind and body doubled the amount which assembled during all of their past interactions.

Did fresh grief pertaining to Ella's unforeseen death direct this excitement to fill voids complicated by heavy sorrow riddled with confusion?

Or did realizing that she was finally liberated from an egotistical husband, who showed how he cared very little, compel her to feel remarkably rhapsodic?

Perhaps the answer pertained to both.

Hunger-

Lust-

Pleasure-

Consolation.

Each of these things churned within her like some severe storm brewing.

She dragged her nails across the back of his neck when growling, "Goddammit, fuck me."

Karsyn remained silent. His mind continued to repeat those things he did to Ella last night while holding the belt secured around her throat. This remembrance of aggression kept up his motivation to treat Blair with hostility.

She gasped for air.

And then paused from stroking his dick and pinched beneath its head again.

Her mind wandered off track from things taking place at the moment. The setting she entered was dark and quiet. Advancing from wherever she entered, her body still reminded her of all the awesome sensations caused by Karsyn outside the realm of memory. Although it was bizarre to incorporate these delectable components within the existence of her imagined self, she believed opposing circumstances catered to various degrees of passion that intertwined both worlds to be very near one in the same.

Interior darkness directed her to a familiar place. Somewhere that could possibly ignite dread in a person if they caught even as little as a momentary glimpse of the site that she uncannily infringed.

Blair stood beside the bed that was vaguely visible in the dark. She saw what she expected to stumble upon and that was Ella still sleeping from being heavily intoxicated, but what she did not anticipate was finding her private areas broadcast for all to see. Right then and there she interpreted that someone had come before her and robbed Ella of her potential purity. Blair did assume that her daughter was respectful enough to not partake in such shenanigans; of course, this suspected decency didn't appear to be the case anymore. There were two warm dicks in the house that would love nothing more than to bleed out a piece of virgin puss. One of those cocks was mindful of the fact that Ella wasn't capable of physically or mentally responding to any improper behavior.

Her honest opinion was that Cody had come into Ella's room at some point during the night and sexually violated her - knowing that she'd have no recollection of the crime committed against her. He did always check her out in an odd way when she flaunted her little ass in clothing that left nothing for the imagination to ponder. He made borderline sexual references toward her on occasion also. The main reason she suspected him was because of that shamefully jaw-dropping content she discovered of Ella on his phone. He'd been viewing lurid photos and watching objectified videos of a double life that Blair didn't know her daughter was facilitating.

She seriously doubted that Karsyn carried the same evil in his blood to perpetrate a rape. He never really paid Ella much attention. The few times that he did all pertained to ordinary everyday matters and weren't made into uncomfortable situations like his father was good for doing. Accompanying his portrayal of innocence was the subsistence that he and Blair were romantically involved and had been a secret item now for almost a year. If he had ever taken an interest in Ella, then she believed that he would have made a comment or did something instinctually for her to recognize the red flag.

She didn't hold Ella accountable for what might have happened and she wasn't necessarily pissed at her either, but she was sickened by the idea of Ella going as far as she did for the men's attention. Ella was barely an adult yet she advertised herself as if she had knowledge in knowing how to satisfy the desires of men. Despite being disgusted by her daughter's unsuitable lifestyle, she wasn't exactly jealous since her relationship with Karsyn provided more excitement than any one night she experienced in two marriages.

But she did arrive at Ella's bed driven by motive nonetheless.

Blair held her accountable for destabilizing her marriage to Cody. There was no way that parading her little sweet tart body had nothing to do with him distancing himself. The ultimate threat was if she discovered a way to entice Karsyn and then steer him away from his faithfulness to Blair. Even if he didn't react physically to Ella's advances, Blair didn't want to risk the temptation of dirty thoughts encouraging him to do something.

Seeing Ella in this condition after an apparent sexual assault gave her the confidence required to perpetrate the grisly objective that brought her here. No one would suspect a devoted mother of gruesomely eliminating her daughter; especially when that mother was expecting her second child. But a lot of questionable matters did add up for authorities to aim their suspicion at the sexually driven stepfather whose darkest secret pertained to the victim. Cody may not have known but he created the basis for making himself the prime suspect.

Blair raised her hand and admired the polished metal piece barely glinting in vague moonlight. Tilting it at various angles to catch glimpses of two lengthy spikes, she became joyously overwhelmed by the notion that the BBQ fork would serve its duty in successfully terminating the adversary.

She growled as her mind continued replaying the incident at the same time that Karsyn's fingers prolonged treating her with reckless infringement. Her emotional eroticism advanced to initiate her first orgasm. She didn't actually want to cream this way but the sensation was too exhilarating to ignore.

She revisited those long tines penetrating Ella's flesh. Her mind painted by bloodshed inspired a feverish groan to bestow the room.

"Now!" she gasped, turning her head toward him and rubbing her lips up and down the side of his face.

"*DNA…*"

"*Warrant for collection.*"

Detective Roismann's burdensome voice resumed mortifying Karsyn's intellect.

He ripped away from her and it was a difficult detachment that came with excruciating discomfort since she never disengaged on her own, but he did distance himself and stood ahead of the bed.

He didn't have to say anything for her to notice that something was seriously wrong. She recognized the unsettlement just by his expression.

"Karsyn, what's going on?" she asked, struggling to breathe while agitated for getting rejected unexpectedly.

"This is wrong," he spluttered.

Of course, he couldn't tell her the real reason why he withdrew.

The incentive to drop back came from knowing that the police had nothing on his father. It would not have mattered if they found Cody covered from head to toe in Ella's blood because the most damning piece of evidence belonged to Karsyn. Sure, his father wasn't going to refuse submitting to a DNA swab since he had nothing to hide. The police would discover that the semen inside Ella did not belong to him and then they would approach Karsyn as the next in line to provide a sample. They fucking had him and there was nothing he could do to avoid the outcome. Not only was Blair's trust in him going to dissolve and their relationship come to an abrupt end, but her greatest concern would still exist. She didn't know now but would soon realize that she was going to remain entangled in the despair of having to endure an undesired marriage. What Karsyn found most upsetting was the idea that Cody would go on raising his child under the assumption that it was his own - all while possibly never having the truth revealed to him.

"What do you mean?" Blair questioned, distinctly puzzled. "I don't understand. We've been doing this for a long time. How is it not okay all of a sudden?"

"Because Ella's dead!" he snapped. "And it bothers me that this is all you can think about right now."

"It is not the only thing I'm thinking about. You have no idea of the things that's been on my mind since finding her this morning. I'm terrified. My thoughts are everywhere. The only thing I want is for you to be here for me," she said.

"I am here for you, okay? I just don't feel like this is the right thing to do with everything that's going on," he stated.

"All I want you to do is make me feel better," she said, prior to sitting up slowly and scooting near the edge of the bed. "Come here."

"Listen to yourself," he advised, taking several steps in one direction and then back in front of her again. "Getting my dick inside you really is all that you can think about."

While her interest obviously lingered on having him intimately involved, Karsyn was completely turned off. There was no way he could maintain emotional arousal alongside dread devouring his mind. The urge to confess that he fucked his own stepsister but had no involvement with her murder came close to the tip of his tongue, but he couldn't come clean about the matter because he knew that she'd not believe everything. If he admitted to having sex with Ella, then it would be natural for Blair to assume that he killed her too. There was a policeman not too far outside the room and the last thing he needed was for her to rip the door open in a fit of rage and proclaim that he was the one responsible.

Karsyn started pacing in front of the bed again. He didn't have a goddamn clue pertaining to what he should do.

He loved Blair and refused to jeopardize the bond they shared. Of course, the truth would become clear to everyone when the DNA analysis came back and not only cleared his father but also forced him to be subpoenaed to take the same test - which he'd ultimately fail. Telling her the truth or waiting until his sample exposed him, both would emulate the same damning conclusion. He was going to be apprehended for first-degree murder and his father freed to preside over the perfect little family that should have been his to claim.

He paced faster.

The pandemonium associated with his dreary anticipation of things to come had him timidly dreading the hours ahead.

"What the hell is wrong with you?" Blair asked. "You're acting like a lunatic and it's starting to creep the shit out of me."

He glimpsed at her and was able to feel the cold expression excrete from his face. As much as he loved Blair and didn't want to lose her, there did come that brief thought about doing something he never believed would cross his mind. The idea that crept inside his soul regarded the concept that if he was going to pay for a crime he didn't commit, then he might as well justify the inevitable conviction. He flirted with the notion so much that he carefully visualized placing his hands around her throat and strangling the life out of her and his unborn child. Ridding their existence would eliminate his misery of dwelling on the detail of his father flourishing in the family life while he resided behind bars.

His leg twitched as if his body was prepared to commit the act while his mind still debated.

"Sit with me and calm down," she insisted.

Karsyn looked away from her and glanced all around the side of the room without focusing on one particular area. He didn't want to give her any more attention since all that he could picture was murdering her in order to preserve their chemistry.

"Please, Karsyn, don't do this to me," she pleaded, pressing one hand against her stomach and attempting to move off the bed.

He took one step toward her before reaching ahead and violently shoving her back down just as she was about to stand up all the way. Blair winced and grabbed her belly with both hands. Perhaps a substantial amount of pain sprang throughout her inside when her body jolted unexpectedly in an unfamiliar way.

"You know what?!" she burst out angrily. "Fuck you! When all of this is over and we get back home, then you can pack your shit and leave. No man is ever going to lay a hand on me like you just did."

He pointed a stern finger at her. "I would not advise you to test me right now," he warned, replaying brief fragments of the make-believe strangulation in his head.

Her mouth opened as though she was ready to speak again.

"Don't," he advised.

Her lips came together.

Struggling to clear his mind from the intrusive thought, he ridiculously scanned the far side of the room once more and honed in on the only other door that was not the one through which they entered. Deep down, he knew that he couldn't harm her because he cared too much. Intensifying panic and gut wrenching stress contributed to his sudden decision to bolt away from the bed.

"I can't do this with you!" he yelped somberly.

Blair remained silent. She could feel her face crumple with confusion while watching him storm across the room. Wondering what was wrong with him did not cross her mind. Maybe she assumed the stress surrounding everything that had happened finally became too much and caused him to snap.

Karsyn rushed the door open.

He turned the light on.

Then he leaped inside the room and slammed the door shut by pressing his back against it.

He noticed his nerves were completely shot because he felt himself trembling all over. His chest ached and it was difficult to breathe. So many thoughts ran through his head that it was almost impossible to concentrate on just one. Everything from Jake's provocation to suck his dick to briefly witnessing violent bloodshed when passing Ella's doorway, and those damning words spoken by Detective Roismann's ever present voice; all of these things blended together to form the impression that they occurred at once.

"Fuck me," he whined, processing the realization that the relationship with Blair was over despite his innocence. He was as good as guilty because no one was going to believe him anyway.

He was destined to spend the rest of his life amongst the true coldblooded murderers of the world.

And he'd likely serve as a victim of continuous sexual assault himself.

He twisted the locking mechanism on the doorknob before stepping forward and slouching in front of the sink to check his reflection in the mirror. Tension and fear, both really did a number on him. If he didn't understand the severity of his emotional chaos, then the discombobulation anchored in his eyes would have definitely signaled its intensity. Aside from the madman gaze reflecting back at him, he recognized that his immense anxiety glazed him with sweat - leaving him to resemble his worst days as a strung out junkie.

"I can't-" He turned the cold water on. "I am not going down for this shit."

Karsyn leaned down and splashed a few handfuls of water on his face. He raised and checked himself in the mirror again. Water may have washed the sweat away but it failed to rinse off the mold of discontent. He looked at the wire rack mounted on the wall above the toilet next to the sink and targeted a couple of neatly prepared white towels on the shelf above matching washcloths and two individually packaged miniature soap bars. Then he glanced further to his right and observed the metal rod which supported the shower curtains.

His mind suddenly stumbled onto a dark path where the absence of hindsight offered no return. The notion of prison life gnawing at his conscience soon sent him plummeting into misery never before charted in his life.

He grabbed one of the towels, unfolded it, and laid it inside the sink. Once the cloth absorbed water beyond the point of being able to withstand holding any more, he pulled the towel from the sink and began to twist it around itself to expel excess water. Whatever had crossed his mind, it seemed unorthodox based on this latest action.

Blair remained at the foot of the bed and listened carefully as the faint sound of running water poured into the room from beyond the door. "Karsyn, are you okay?!" she called out.

He didn't answer.

She scooted back slowly toward the headboard and positioned herself on one side. Then she turned and sat facing the edge. Having both feet on the floor helped to eliminate whatever possible strains she might have felt when reaching for the corded phone on the bedside table. She picked up the handset and thought for a moment before proceeding to dial a particular number on her mind. Pressing every necessary digit on the dial pad with a slight pause between strikes, Blair eyed the bathroom door not too far from her position.

Her mind wandered instantly.

The place she'd been taken was murky. She stood just inches in front of a closed door in a dark hallway. Her hand gripped its knob but she appeared rather reluctant to turn the handle. Perhaps she experienced much preset dread about what she might discover after opening the door. Her gut feeling did assure her that something foul was awaiting visual recognition. She did not want to accept that something iniquitous was taking place but she couldn't ignore her suspicion.

She remembered that twisting the knob and then pushing the door open may have taken a matter of seconds but felt like five minutes. She didn't thrust the door too far - only enough to get a slim view of the one thing she had hoped not to find out. The room wasn't provided much light; however, Blair did vaguely recognize the identity of the man standing inside the room was strikingly similar to Karsyn. Unfortunately, he wasn't all that she noticed. Sprawled out on the bed in front of him was Ella. Blair didn't have to see her face to know that it was her daughter; she was one-hundred percent positive that it was Ella because everything was taking place in her bedroom.

Turmoil struck Blair and chewed at her while she observed him carrying out an unspeakable act. She could not believe that he'd stoop so low to take advantage of an unconscious young lady. Plus he confessed his love for her so many times to convince her that he was nothing like the predator presented in front of her now.

Delirium broiled inside her and the urge to burst into the room and confront him was momentous, but she found it in herself to preserve, somehow, after placing her hand on the door in preparation to storm inside. Underneath all her anger and disappointment, she pulled together a style of collectivism stemming from the long awaited opportunity to change the entire course of direction involving her life.

Her thoughts shifted to revisit the moment that she pulled the blanket down with just one elbow and smeared Ella's blood that was on her hands all across Cody's chest as he slept.

Then she replayed the moment when she stashed the grill fork under his side of the bed. Of course, the police would surely uncover it during their investigation but she didn't hide it with the intent of not being located. She simply believed that placing it barely out of sight would go a long way in shifting all suspicion on him. It would also increase the chance of the authorities finding her story credible. The idea of her fingerprints being all over the handle did cross her mind but she didn't stress over the fact because it would be natural for her prints and anyone else's in the household to be present. Since she was pretty much the only one that washed dishes regularly, she had a justifiable reason that could not be questioned.

She tapped the last digit to make an outgoing call and listened as the line transitioned from silent to ringing.

Karsyn tied the second waterlogged towel to the first one that he had fastened around the curtain rod and then pulled it to make sure that both knots were capable of withstanding weight. Neither of the knots came loose or gave any indication that they might. Believing that they were snug enough to follow through with their responsibility, he turned his back to the tub without thinking twice about what he was going to do. Honestly, there wasn't enough room in his head to second guess himself right now. The troublesome thought that he would soon become a cellblock meat puppet, violated and passed along from one hepatitis infected deviant to the next, consumed his mind. The deliverance of a twenty one year old male in the state penitentiary would be ripe fruit for men that spent the majority of their lonesome nights jacking off with useless hands. Thinking about how he willfully submitted himself as an oral fleshlight to Jake's perverse debauchery filled him with nausea and dread. He couldn't imagine the amount of catastrophic disgust he might endure if he was tossed inside the steel cage as some fuckboy for a pedigree of agonistic miscreants.

He looked at water which he didn't shut off from flowing out of the faucet but couldn't hear it strike inside the sink because all the madness swarming within his head was overwhelmingly loud. Nothing about the exterior world registered with him; the repetitive interior derangement stole those basic percipiences.

Karsyn stepped up backwards onto the side of the bathtub and his other foot followed pursuit. He grabbed the rope of towels dangling beside him and raised the loose end beneath his chin. Then he pulled the towel against his throat and wrapped it around him twice before making a third knot on the back of his neck. He touched his throat to check for slack and was pleased to discover that he couldn't slip his fingers between the towel and himself. He did suspect that he wouldn't achieve this attempt beforehand, because the cloth pressed snug against his windpipe and caused difficulty breathing.

He channeled his attention to the door in front of him and seemed to have lost awareness that Blair was waiting for him on the other side. Realistically, there was too much internal clutter for him to revert to the current moment and all that it retained. His mind kept displacing him to relive the situation that involved him sitting in Jake's car. The event resurrected itself so vividly that he could almost taste the body cheese flavor of sweaty cock while imaginary dirt particles crunched between his teeth when he bit down. He fought to clear his thoughts but there was no escaping this eroticized hell.

His tear glands produced excess fluid which made it difficult to see his surroundings, but those watery eyes weren't the result of sadness; actually, the buildup was a result of outrage toward allowing himself to descend to such ignominious standards.

With a mind absent of rationality, Karsyn shuffled his heels to the very edge of the bathtub. Nothing mattered at this point - even the excitement for his unborn child had fizzled out below the nonsensical contribution of mental whispers encouraging him that there was no point to continue onward in life.

Liquid insult came forward and drizzled down his face at the same time that he shut his eyes.

He shuffled forward again - not much - still, it was enough to follow through with what he'd come to carry out.

The towels pulled tight, instantly choking him, and the back of his feet smacked the side of the bathtub before his legs thrashed wildly - creating a racket that likely spewed past the door and into the motel room. Several times, he kicked the toilet and attempted landing one foot on the lid to prevent hanging himself but he was in such an awkward position that he couldn't gain stable support even if he wanted. Determination played a role also; he didn't want to *actually* save himself. His dedication to dispose of unalterable affliction quickly contributed to him pulling away from the toilet and leaving his legs dangling without seeking the opportunity for another chance at life.

His airway had been denied oxygen for far too long.

The sound of choking depleted to just a constant wheeze which almost pitched no sound at all.

Lightheadedness turned into acute disorientation.

Karsyn didn't only feel his life fading-

He celebrated the notion that he might finally encounter peace amongst the chaos.

Four long rings stumbled into Blair's ear before the line went silent.

"Hello?" she whispered immediately.

Male voice: "Why are you calling me? You're going to blow the cover on everything."

She glanced at the bathroom door. "It's okay. I think he knows that he doesn't have any options because he's literally out of his fucking mind. He's been in the bathroom for a bit now, and I think he might be doing what I thought he'd do."

"*If he isn't?*"

"Karsyn isn't exactly like his father. He doesn't handle shit well. If he's not scared enough to fix the situation on his own, then it's no big deal. We'll go with Plan B. With my story and your testimony, father and son will go to hell together," she said.

"*You do know I'm not okay with your little backup plan, right?*"

She scoffed and rolled her eyes. "I don't understand you at times. You're in a position where no one is going to doubt what you say. All that you've got to do is address that you observed him behaving strangely and making cryptic comments, then I'll follow up by stating what you said as being true. It's pretty simple, Jerek. Seriously, though, I don't see us having to worry about Plan B, but it's there if we need it."

"*Things will be less complicated if I'm not dragged into the middle.*"

Blair laughed sarcastically. "You're overreacting. None of this is complicated. We have the perfect plan and every part of it is flawless."

"*Overreacting? You've created the most fucked up triangle I've ever known. Attaching my name isn't going to be good for us in the long run.*"

"Oh stop. We're not going-"

A dial tone blared in her ear when the recipient ended the call unannounced.

"Hey," she snapped quietly.

Only the lingering dial tone provided a response.

"Jarek," she spoke, despite not having him on the line.

BAM! BAM! BAM!

Three harsh knocks slammed the motel door.

The unexpected disruption jounced Blair and she hung up the phone immediately. Raising off the bed was a different story, since she was dealing with a swollen belly that caused specific limitations. She stood slowly which appeared to legitimately validate that her circumstantial short term physical disabilities were not deceitful acts like everything else she portrayed about herself lately.

BAM! BAM!

She held the bottom of her stomach and scampered at a pace that nearly exceeded her capabilities. She realized how much she almost outdid herself when she reached the door and had to take a moment to catch her breath as slight discomfort paraded throughout her abdomen. Sucking down a few deep breaths lessened the severity of such botheration and she finally managed to proceed with opening the door. Her eyes widened as though she was taken by shock. Apparently, she did not anticipate this unforeseen incident.

Officer Ryve glanced at her just for a moment before surveying the room. "I assume he's locked himself in the bathroom?" he asked curiously.

She stepped aside, making the entryway accessible. "Seems that way. He's been in there for a while."

He crossed the doorway and continued onward into the room. His placid demeanor wasn't necessarily peculiar, though, Blair expected him to barge in under protocol; meaning that she figured he would've entered with his weapon drawn and prepared to confront the unexpected. He strolled leisurely with his hands on his hips while whistling a terrible tune instead.

She shut the door.

Crek.

The lock barely pitched a sound.

She turned and recognized him studying the bed intently when passing in front of it. Seeing only half his scrunched face was sufficient in admitting his confusion.

"You've been grieving so much that he had to hold you?" he asked.

She glanced at the bed and instantly noticed what caught his attention; the blanket wasn't just wrinkled from her and Karsyn laying on it but their impressions were still scarcely visible on the mattress.

"I needed the comfort," she stated, creeping away from the door. "And it was a smart move letting him know I'm the closest thing to him."

Officer Ryve stepped in front of the bathroom door and gripped the handle of his holstered weapon before knocking twice.

Karsyn didn't respond.

He tried again, knocking once.

"I'm telling you that he's not going to answer," Blair mouthed.

After a long silent moment, Officer Ryve glanced over his shoulder at her. "Did you bother to try checking on him?" he asked.

She shook her head and shrugged.

"Well…?" he lashed out - clearly insinuating that not getting answered by one person was about all that he could tolerate.

"No," she mumbled softly. 'He went so crazy that I didn't want to compromise my wellbeing.''

Officer Ryve attempted twisting the knob but it would not turn since Karysn had locked the door. Putting his ear to what he assumed was cheap hollow wood, he heard only the faint noise of water flowing.

"Sounds like he turned the water on to create a distraction for you not to hear whatever he set out to do," he presumed.

"See?!" she exclaimed, extraordinarily chirpy. "I knew from the start he wasn't equipped to take on the risks. He did exactly what I knew he would."

Officer Ryve lowered his hand off the gun. Perhaps common knowledge instilled the confidence in him to understand that Karysn most likely did aspire for an end to life.

"How long has he been in there?" he asked.

"I don't know the exact length of time. All I can say is it's been a while," she replied.

"Well, I've got to get in there to see what's up with him. If he's got a pulse but isn't alert, then that's going to require a hospital visit with some recovery time before he's able to be questioned. He can be arrested while in medical care but our entire process gets slowed down. If he's done what is necessary to cease having a heartbeat, then enacting your idea of Plan B is one less stress I'll have to worry about," he disclosed.

"Just leave him for now," she rattled. "We've waited on this moment for how long - thirteen months, at best?"

Officer Ryve turned his back to the door and immediately sighted the depth of lovesickness in sad eyes staring at him from the nearest corner of the bed. Despite seeing what he believed was her reverence for him, he felt that he needed further validation and so he questioned, "Are you truly in love with me or am I another piece of the configuration in this big scheme you've orchestrated?"

"No, Jarek! I did this for you. For us," she declared. "Why would you even think to ask me that?"

Officer Jarek Ryve sighed noisly, as if aggravated by ongoing ineludible thoughts. "You're married. You've slept in the same bed with your husband every night. You fucked your stepson - more times than I'll ever want to know - got pregnant, and convinced the kid that he's the father. I've been nothing but a side piece in this mess, so I do sometimes question if what we have means anything to you. I hate to admit it, but there have been some pretty dire moments that I've doubted I'm the father. It's a toss up, Blair."

Her confident posture degenerated once she mindfully digested his uncongenial words. "I did what I felt was necessary. Me and you could not be together if I didn't come up with a viable plan. It wouldn't matter how often I expressed my unhappiness, Cody would have been adamant about not granting me a divorce. I'm property in his mind. When it comes to Karsyn, having him involved was the only way to guarantee my freedom. I've made this look like a father and son partnership; however, the father got jealous of his son banging their obsession and took it upon himself to eliminate her."

Jarek glowered at her with incertitude. "Remind me to never cross your bad side. You're nefarious as fuck. Manipulative. Not the breed of woman I'd ordinarily get myself involved with."

She sneered. "I'm not going to formulate any wrongdoings against you. This was just a situation that I had to resourcefully weasel myself away from. Cody and Karsyn could not have set themselves up any better. Motive and evidence are stacked against them. Ella, well, she basically sacrificed herself as my scapegoat. I am bothered that she gave her life for me to escape but she didn't feel anything. I didn't think I'd feel this much aftershock since I knew she was heading down a path that probably would have landed some random dick to leave her dead in an alley anyway. We both know it was only a matter of time before amateur porn would've led to prostitution."

"You butchered your fucking daughter, it should bother you," he noted.

Blair smiled. "I could cry, really, but at the same time I know we've got a new life to celebrate and start over with again. And yes, Jarek, this is your child. I kept track of everything I did. Me and Karsyn weren't fooling around during the time I got pregnant, and I sure as hell wasn't getting anything from Cody. You're the only person I'd been with when I found out."

Jarek nodded. "I do not doubt that you carefully calculated every step. Not sure how long it took you to piece all of this together but you made certain it was done in a way to keep your hands clean."

She giggled connivingly. "When you spend every day thinking up all sorts of scenarios, the imagination eventually gives you something solid to go on."

He stepped away from the door and approached her at the edge of the bed. "We've still got to keep this relationship strictly between us for a while. Maybe the next six months. Last thing we need is one of the guys in the department to see or hear that we're together while things are fresh."

"Oh, I agree. It'll also make it seem I had plenty of time to grieve," she added.

"Like you're seriously going to cry over spilled milk when it was you that knocked the glass off the table," he stated.

She bowed her head at him and smirked rather naughtily. "Only time you're going to hear me whine is when this baby decides to pop. Sucks you're not going to see it but you'll be the first person I call when I get out of labor."

He stopped in front of her and raised her head after pressing his fingers beneath her chin. Then he reached behind her waist and pulled. Her stomach rammed hard against him and remained under pressure since he didn't let up squeezing her.

"Or you could call the station and say you need an officer's assistance. Just text me in advance after the contraptions start so that I can make sure I'm the one that takes the call," he mentioned.

"That works too," she whispered, bringing both hands on the front of his tactical belt. "How much time do you think we have?"

"Umm-" He glanced toward the ceiling for a moment and considered how to respond instead of blurting out the first thought that came to mind. "Detective Roismann is very thorough in how he handles matters. He'll leave nothing unturned for a piece of evidence. My guess is that we've got a couple of more hours."

"Good," she purred, and then began unfastening the belt. "I want you to have your way with me."

Those nine little words invoked a sudden reaction.

He grabbed the sides of her shirt and yanked upward, clearing her body before tearing it off her head and tossing it on the floor. Her tits were secured in a dull pink bra and they appeared smaller than he remembered them, but her stomach wasn't this large when he last saw it either. The breasts were pretty much sitting on top of her stomach. He recalled the last time he fondled them there was plenty of room to bounce them around during foreplay. Despite the unexpected shock triggered by her marginally unattractive proportions, Jarek clenched a handful of one entire breast and pinched it with a firm grip. Blair groaned while he squeezed but she did not resist.

He removed lengths of hair dangling on the side of her face and stashed them behind her ear. Afterward, he swooped down and made contact with her mouth. The taste of her kisses was one thing he'd gone too long without and he pried more than half his tongue past her teeth to scoop out the forgotten flavor.

She temporarily stripped him of his profession and surrendered him to his vulnerabilities by dropping his belt. Then she unfastened his pants and ripped the uniform shirt from staying tucked. Kissing blinded her but she did manage to quickly undo his shirt one button at a time.

She broke from his lips and gasped, "Goddammit, fuck me."

Jarek forced himself on her mouth again. Between tasting her tongue and biting her lip, he felt the desire to consume her in every way possible was intensifying. He arranged the two of them with her back facing the bed. Blair reached inside the unbuttoned shirt and dragged her nails down his chest. Both of them expressing equal hunger elevated their intimacy to playful aggression. She drove her nails deeper against his skin until a trail of red whelps followed her moving down; Jarek bit her lip harder each time and crushed the breast which caused enough discomfort that she grunted - bringing him to suck in and recycle her heavily expelled breath.

He pulled away from her mouth, hissing as her fingernails scratched along his stomach. She almost reached the top of his boxers when he abruptly stopped her by shoving her backwards on the bed. The jarring force resulted in her whimpering but then she smiled after. Perhaps she actually enjoyed the rough treatment of him not showing sympathy for the additional life developing within. Karsyn always treated her like some package scheduled for delivery; fragile and handled with care. Getting treated gently wasn't bad but she preferred that a man exert his strength and dominance in the bedroom. Jarek's natural ability to satisfy her preference was the reason why every encounter they shared was a memorable experience.

As she laid in front of him, sensually heated and unsure what he might do next, he reached on her sides and pulled down her pants and panties together at the same time. He expressed total disregard for her clothing when he stretched them out beneath her knees and then shoved them to her feet. Shedding them from her legs wasn't a grueling task but he followed through with assertiveness anyway before slinging them over his shoulder across the room. Then he placed his hands on the inside of her knees and forced her legs open.

Blair could not see herself but she knew she was laying exactly the same as Ella when discovered. This morbid realization quickly turned into a bizarre fascination that proved sentimentally invigorating. As if blood spilled upon Ella's body was some artistically macabre exhibit of death professing that it, too, could orgasm, Blair felt the grisly aftermath fresh in her mind was more than alluring. The powerful sense of liberation gave her a tremendous adrenaline rush. Escaping that miserably unappealing lifestyle as a neglected housewife provided her the dignity to suspect she might finally rekindle happiness that avoided her for so long. She'd no longer have to worry about not feeling attractive or be forced to go out of her way to please others while receiving nothing in return. Jarek eliminated her insecurities without having to do anything spectacular. He likely assumed that her hips squirming while she groaned was due to him touching her in a way that drove her crazy, but the actual harvesters of her concupiscence were self-neglected characteristics - psychopathy and narcissism - which she advocated denying existence.

The true villain was someone else.

Always.

Misguided and emotionally oppressed Blair could never find things most important to her in a man; however, she trusted Jarek retained such attributes that were lacking in her eventual past two marriages.

He scraped his tongue up her inner thigh and reached the pit of her crotch, where he smelled the smothering reek of stagnant puss without sniffing. He wasn't aware that Karsyn rubbed her wet just a short while ago; therefore, he might have guessed the foul fragrance resided because she hadn't freshened herself to be presentable since yesterday. Regardless of what he took into consideration, he made his way to the center between her legs and scrubbed his tongue against viscid textured skin that was bitter tasting due to the drying of prior arousal. It wasn't a flavor he'd ever tasted on her but he didn't seem to mind since his tongue sank almost as deep as it did while they kissed. When he wasn't battering the inside of her vagina, then he alternated between slurping and sucking its lips.

She suddenly succumbed to her back bending off the bed and endured rapid chills bolting up her spine at the exact moment he grazed the perineum and licked further down near her asshole. Receiving attention on this commonly avoided region did thrust her into a frenzy, and she had spent her entire adult life not knowing the extent of erogenous pleasure it provided until Jarek came along. Her first husband wasn't very explorative. Cody was only concerned about pleasing himself. Karsyn did satisfy her under basic conditions; unfortunately, he was too fundamental in the sense that he never attempted anything new. Jarek, on the other hand, was the fucking jackpot!

After her body settled enough following the initial frenzy, and she adjusted herself flush on the bed again, Blair raised her head and looked down with fascination to watch him in action but all she saw was the overgrown protrusion in her belly blocking the view. She laid her head back down, shut her eyes, and engaged her mind to bounce back and forth from the current situation to a disarranged parade of memories. About a dozen times her and Karsyn fucked ran together and played out in a matter of seconds; periodic glimpses of plunging the BBQ fork into Ella's mutilated torso flashed in the thick of her taking the dick. Brief peeks of Cody getting escorted by police out of the house presented themselves also. Altogether these sights magnified the effects brought on by Jarek eating her out.

She could not lay still.

She couldn't be quiet.

He receded from dunking his head against her groin and stood between her legs, towering high above with evidence of having a go at oral satisfaction lustering around his mouth. Blair looked up and saw cringe-fueled wrinkles of revulsion scattered throughout leathery skin on the middle-aged face of a man who came across as being more eager to please than have his wishes met. Numbed by the state of enjoyment, she took much pride in acknowledging his disenchantment because it settled well with all the twistedly sick filth stirring inside her.

Unable to see everything he was doing since her belly was in the way, she did notice him slightly bend over before hearing his pants jingle while presumably sliding down his legs. Jarek reached under her knees and towed her closer onto the edge of the bed. She screeched when getting dragged because he conquered her with an accentuated rage that engulfed her secretly sadistic thirsts. Placing one hand on her stomach and squeezing with no concern for the life inside, he reached down and guided himself into her spoiled cunt.

She gasped, sensing every portion of his stout penis dive inside. She didn't often think about it but he was more firm and larger than Karsyn. His thrusts struck a spot that made purring irresistible.

He felt that she wasn't entirely aroused at the moment, and the little bit of sogginess spread upon her crotch resulted from his tongue, but it didn't stop him from pounding the meat pocket like he would if she was completely turned on. Her constant howls and scrunched face indicated that she wasn't exactly having the best time, which gave him every reason to believe this might go down as her most memorable encounter.

Of all the things he didn't know…

Blair moaned and winced but she absolutely adored the opportunity to feel like her whore daughter - obsessed over, and ultimately taken.

As if her vagina came naturally equipped with a shutter button, her mind jumped from imagining one scenario to another every time the tip of his dick poked the cervix. Although she didn't know precisely what happened to Karsyn, she found it amusing and strangely stimulating to suspect possibilities. She locked eyes with Jarek while terrible images worked wonders on her sexual appetite.

Karsyn slouched on the floor between the bathtub and toilet. His left arm extended inside the tub, and the last remaining beads of blood dripped from the laceration on his wrist and dribbled into the puddle overlaying the floor of the tub. In his other hand was a jagged piece of bloodstained glass that was obviously used to slice himself open after breaking the mirror above the sink.

"Ah- Dammit. Fuck yeah!" she squalled, fidgeting all over while Jarek continued giving it to her rough.

The next depiction showed that Karsyn had drowned himself in the tub full of water.

She didn't know exactly how he brought closure to his issues but she was pretty damn certain that he found a way, because he totally lost his shit before vanishing for what became too long.

While Karsyn's corpse dangled from the rope of towels, Jarek felt that penetrating Blair suddenly came with unexpected ease. The sloshing sound of their private parts making music together probably convinced him that he hit the precise area to make her crotch drool. This quick outcome caused him to aim at hitting the same spot with the exact adversarial pace. He didn't know the extent of the effect in connection with her lusts for bloodshed and violent death; she literally *got off* reminiscing about what she had done, and caused Karsyn to do.

Imagining herself as Ella, she looked at Jarek and envisioned him with slut blood smeared across his unbuttoned shirt, face, and hands.

"Choke me!" she pleaded desperately.

Compelled to satisfy her wildest desires, he grabbed her narrow throat and pressed down before squeezing. She gagged as soon as her airway was clamped. The voluntary threat to her survival induced her to orgasmically cream on the bed, and she accepted that it might be the one time in her life she squirted.

At last those derelict qualities in her furtively estranged personality discovered their intent was to bring delectation to every dull angle of her substance. All characteristics strewn together for the first time shed light on the fact that matters pertaining to previous events weren't ramifications of a random occurrence.

They were attributes that existed, dormant, calmly awaiting the opportunity to unbosom her true identity and benefit from situational manipulation.

Andre Sanders is an author residing in Christiansburg, Virginia. HER ONLY FAN is his first work outside of the horror genre. His splatterpunk revenge short story HEN HOUSE became an Amazon bestseller upon release. His second novel was adapted into a screenplay. Andre is set to begin his next book, and will deliver unexpected shorts of extreme horror amongst his other works available on Amazon.

www.ingramcontent.com/pod-product-compliance
Lightning Source LLC
Chambersburg PA
CBHW010331140726
47989CB00008BA/3046